KT-578-324

A TOWN CALLED PERDITION

Jesse 'Mav' Bolder heads into Pure Water, known as Perdition because of its evil reputation. There he encounters some very shady characters, among them the sheriff, Bill Bronco, and local rancher Bunce and his hired killers. But there are good people in Pure Water too and when Mav befriends them, Sheriff Bronco sees it as an opportunity to run them off, leading to a bloody showdown for control of the town.

LEE LEJEUNE

A TOWN CALLED PERDITION

Complete and Unabridged

LINFORD
Leicester

First published in Great Britain in 2012 by
Robert Hale Limited
London

First Linford Edition
published 2014
by arrangement with
Robert Hale Limited
London

A catalogue record for this book is available
from the British Library.

ISBN 978–1–4448–1815–4

1

Mav, alias Jesse Bolder, was riding amidst a sea of cactus plants in the middle of the Arizona desert when he saw something like an oasis ahead. Huckleberry, his horse, pricked up his ears and flared his nostrils expectantly.

'You're damn right, old buddy,' Mav declared. 'There's water ahead and that's the place where we must rest up and have ourselves a refreshing drink.'

Huckleberry tossed his head as though he understood, which he probably did since he and Mav had been together for quite a long spell.

Mav twitched the reins with his left hand and the horse inclined towards the green junipers ahead.

'Hold on there, good buddy,' Mav said, reining in suddenly, no doubt to Huck's disapproval. The rider dismounted and looked down. 'What's this, then?' he said.

What he saw was a lop-sided board hanging somewhat precariously from a post. The words were amateurishly painted but quite distinct. They spelled out: THIS IS THE WAY TO PERDITION. There was a blood-red arrow pointing ahead along the trail.

'Perdition,' Mav said to the horse. 'You ever hear of a place called Perdition?'

Huckleberry threw up his head again. He was no doubt thinking of that fresh cooling water rather than perdition.

'What's perdition anyways?' Mav muttered to himself. It was a long time since he had been at school. So words like perdition hadn't come up too frequently.

Huckleberry snorted and moved restlessly to one side.

'OK, old buddy, you know best,' Mav agreed. He mounted up again and rode on down a slow incline towards where he heard the distinct tinkling of flowing water. 'Yep, that's good spring water,' he said to the horse, but Huckleberry needed no telling; he was way ahead of his rider and dreaming of something like horse's heaven.

It was a good spot down by the riverside and Mav relieved Huck of his burdens and let him go for the drink he needed so much. Huck raised his head and whinnied and plunged his nose into the water. Mav lowered his canteen into the stream and filled it full of pristine water. There wasn't much for Huck to eat but what there was would have to do. Mav too was a little stretched for food but he had beans and Arbuckle, so he would be OK until he shot a deer or a jack-rabbit or maybe even a bald eagle, which wasn't very likely anyway.

Mav stretched himself out close to the river and took a doze. It was a long doze and, when he suddenly woke, the sun had gone down behind the junipers and he was staring up at a full moon rising majestically behind the trees. 'That's a real pretty moon,' he said to Huck but the horse was too busy munching the coarse grass under the trees to respond.

'Good as any place to spend the night,'

Mav said. 'I'll just shake the dust off my bones, kindle a little fire and cook up my beans and I do believe I still have a tin of pilchards in stock which is a blessing.'

Mav was a man of method and he soon had a friendly little fire blazing away. He brewed up his Arbuckle, drank a little, and opened his last can of pilchards. 'Pilchards are bigger than sardines,' he said to himself. 'More nourishing too, I daresay.'

He was about to pitch in to his first pilchard when something unexpected happened. A kind of shadow fell across the water and Huck raised his head and looked in Mav's direction, but he wasn't looking at Mav.

Mav went on humming to himself as he slid down his right hand and gripped the Colt Peacemaker in its holster. Then he turned with surprising agility and brought the revolver up level so he could take a shot.

'Steady there!' came a voice from close by.

4

'Steady yourself whoever you are,' Mav replied, cocking the Colt and bringing it up so he could take a shot at the man. 'Maybe you'd be kind enough to lay that shooter you're holding on the ground nice and easy before my trigger finger gets a little nervous.' Mav raised the Colt slightly to emphasize that he meant what he said.

The other man hesitated, trying to make up his mind what to do. Then he bent as if to lay his gun on he ground. This was a critical moment, a moment when a man might become careless. So Mav gestured with the Colt. This might be when a careless man might end up dead!

The other man crouched down and lowered his shooter to the ground. 'Steady there,' he said again. 'Don't get too nervous. A man don't mean no harm.'

Mav gave a low chuckle. 'A man with a gun behind another man's back can mean a lot of harm. Now I want you to leave that peashooter on the ground and come and set yourself down here by the fire nice and easy in case this Colt revolver in my hand gets a little jumpy and shoots you dead. That could be a little inconvenient for both of us, I guess.'

The other man gave a deep throaty chuckle and then rose and approached the fire, leaving his Remington on the ground.

Mav had laid his platter of beans and pilchards to one side. He reached out and picked up the man's revolver. He then spilled out the shells, put them in his pocket, and handed the man his gun. 'Just in case,' he said.

'That ain't no way to treat a friend,' the man said in a high crowing voice.

'And that ain't no way to treat an enemy either,' Mav assured him.

The man was now stretching his hands to the flames. 'I like a man with a sense of humour,' he said. 'Laughter goes a long way in this wilderness, you know that?'

'Could take you to Hell or Perdition,' Mav agreed.

The stranger stretched out a steady hand. 'Jed Arnold,' he said. 'You probably heard tell of me.'

Mav took the hand and pressed down hard. This was another anxious moment. A friend with a firm hand could do some Japanese trick on a man and he might end up on his back or on the fire. But Mav was no weakling and he was beginning to get the measure of the stranger.

'Jed Arnold,' he said. 'I think I've seen a poster somewhere saying you're wanted for a bank robbery, or is my brain playing tricks with me?'

'Probably an old poster,' Arnold replied laconically. 'Anyways, I'm riding the straight trail now. I aim to settle down and become an honest man. I got certain interests close by.'

'Well, that's downright commendable,' Mav said.

'A man don't mean no harm,' Arnold said. 'The world's a hard place, you know. Could I perhaps beg a little of that Arbuckle of yourn?'

'Help yourself and no fancy tricks,' Mav said.

'Tell you what,' Arnold said. 'I got a prairie chicken I caught earlier. I could make it like a peace offering. I see you have pilchards on your plate. Maybe we could do a deal here. I throw in my prairie chicken, you throw in a piece of that there pilchard and a few beans and we could have a real feast here, my friend.'

That sounded reasonable to Mav who was, by nature, a rationalist. So he shrugged. 'OK, bring on the prairie chicken and your horse. I presume you got horseflesh of some kind?'

'I do,' Arnold replied. He rose from the fire so Mav could see him fully. He wore ragged jeans and a somewhat tattered leather vest. His Stetson type hat was somewhat bashed in and he had a brownish beard streaked with grey. Could have been around forty years of age.

Arnold walked away into the woods and Mav thought he might have a

Winchester in a saddle holster up there. He picked up his Colt and checked it just in case Arnold tried something funny with him. But it seemed Arnold was on the level because, after a short spell, he returned leading a somewhat mangy-looking horse and dangling a plucked prairie chicken in his hand.

'OK,' he said, 'Now we can set down and have us a grand feast just as soon as you tell me who you are.'

Mav holstered the Colt and got up off the ground. 'You can call me Mav,' he said.

'Mav,' Arnold reflected, stroking his beard. 'Mav who? Ain't that a woman's name?'

'Not in this case,' Mav said. 'More of a man's name, I would say.'

'Mav what?' Arnold said.

'Just Mav,' Mav replied.

'Mav,' Arnold reflected. 'Heard that name before somewhere.' A little light came into his brown eyes. 'You wouldn't be the Mav who disposed of that Big Bravo bunch back near

Cimarron would ye?'

'That's me,' Mav said. 'Got tangled up with that bunch of hooligans and had to kill most of them. It wasn't a pretty state of affairs and I don't aim to do much in that line again. I don't care for the sight of blood. Makes me feel sort of queasy.'

'Well, you know,' Arnold said, chewing on a mixture of prairie chicken and pilchard, 'As you saw from that old poster, I dun a bit of shooting myself. Nothing much to boast about, but plumb ugly when it happened. A man has to act in self-defence sometimes.'

'To that I agree,' Mav conceded.

Now it was pitch-dark and the big yellow-red moon was pushing itself up higher behind the trees. The two men hobbled the horses so that they couldn't wander off too far. Then they spread their bed-rolls and got ready to sleep.

'Where you headed, anyways?' Arnold asked Mav.

'Nowhere in particular,' Mav said. 'Thought of looking for some kind of work to tide me over. A man needs a little money now and then.'

'What's your line of business?' Arnold enquired.

'Anything I can rustle up, particularly with horses.'

'You could try the MacKinley horse ranch just outside Pure Water.'

'Pure Water,' Mav reflected. 'Would that be 'Perdition'?'

'That's what some call Perdition on account of there are some real low-down characters living there, including the sheriff himself. Bill Bronco. Used to be a prize-fighter, so they say.'

'That so?' Mav said laying out his bed-roll.

'Mind if I sleep here by the fire?' Arnold said. 'It gets kind of cold at night.'

'Sure,' Mav said. 'You can sleep as long as you like just so long as you don't try to sneak up on me during the night with that Winchester of yours, and as long as you don't snore.'

'Never snore. I leave that to the

grizzlies.' Arnold gave a croaking kind of chuckle. Then he rolled himself a quirly and offered his tobacco pouch to Mav. Mav waved it politely away. 'Thanks, but no. I used to, but it makes me cough. So I gave up on it.'

Jed Arnold took off his boots and shook out the dust. Then he snuckered down in his bed-roll and started to snore immediately, not so much like a grizzly but more like a bison.

⋆ ⋆ ⋆

Mav had the rare ability of many travellers and soldiers. He could be awake and asleep at the same time. This meant that, as soon as his head touched the saddle bulking up his bed-roll, he was in the land of dreams. Yet when there was an unusual sound like the breaking of a twig or the rustle of a mouse in the grass, he was as wide awake as a startled deer. So when Jed Arnold rose like a ghost from his bed by the fire during the small hours of the morning, Mav already had his Colt ready.

As Arnold crept towards him, Remington in hand, Mav cocked the Colt and pointed it directly at the approaching figure. Arnold stopped dead immediately and Mav could see him framed in the moonlight breathing heavily.

'You come another step closer and you're dead meat,' Mav said quietly.

Arnold seemed to waver a little. Then he spoke: 'Don't fret yourself, partner. A man has to get up occasionally and take a leak and look around a bit. Stands to reason.'

Mav motioned with his gun. 'Sure. A man takes a leak, he doesn't usually draw his gun and level it at another man.'

'Rattlers,' Arnold said. 'Thought I saw a rattler slithering close to the fire. Fire attracts them varmints. Don't want to be bitten by no rattlers, do we partner?'

'Well now,' Mav said. 'I'm going to make a suggestion here. You put that rattler-shooting weapon of yours down on the ground right where you are.

Then you take your leak somewhere not too close and go back to sleep while I relieve you of that Winchester of yours. Either that or you go out in the woods some place else to sleep.'

Arnold held up his arms in surrender. 'OK, you win, Mr Mav,' he said. Then he went off into the trees to take his leak. After that he came back to the fire and rolled up in his bed-roll again.

'By the way,' Mav said as he took the Winchester. 'You misinformed me about your ability to snore. Next time you go into town make an appointment with the quack. A man snores like you could choke himself to death in his sleep.'

Arnold made no reply. He was already snoring like a wounded buffalo.

2

When the sun peeped up from behind the trees in the east, Mav opened his eyes a little wider. He had been awake for some time and he knew that Jed Arnold was moving about and rustling up the Arbuckle. He was also humming some familiar tune to himself but because his voice was so flat you couldn't quite figure what it could be. As Mav rolled on to his elbow, Arnold came stooping towards him with a tin mug of steaming coffee.

'Thought a man might appreciate a little offering,' he said, 'after last night's misunderstanding, that is.'

'Very welcome too.' Mav accepted the coffee graciously.

Arnold had actually revived the fire so the edge was taken off the chill of the early morning. Mav rolled out of his bed-roll, pulled on his boots and buckled on his gun-belt, leaving Arnold's Remington and Winchester close by his bed-roll. After they had squatted by the fire, rubbing themselves warm, gnawing the bones of the prairie chicken and eating a little jerky, Mav took out his Bowie knife and started a little sawing at the stubble on his cactus jaw.

'I didn't figure you for a shaving man,' Arnold said, peering at him suspiciously from the other side of the fire. Judging by his unkempt beard, he obviously hadn't yet cultivated the habit of regular shaving himself. Scraping off stubble was by no means easy with cold water and without soap and Arnold obviously regarded Mav as some kind of dandified freak. Mav had learned to be simple and methodical. When he had finished the operation he was by no means clean shaven but there was a marked improvement.

'Guess you must be thinking about going in to Perdition,' Arnold croaked.

Mav was putting the finishing touches to his toilette. If it had been a little warmer, he might have stripped off and plunged into the water. But he had the possibility of treachery to consider. So he merely scooped up handfuls of water and threw them on to his face. It was a good way of waking yourself up on a coolish morning. 'Sure, I'm going to Perdition,' he agreed. 'Since I've been on the trail for a week or more it seems the best thing to do.'

''Course it ain't really *Perdition*, not in the real sense of the word as I said last night,' Arnold informed him.

'Like you said, it was Pure Water,' Mav said.

Arnold ran his hand over his brown-grey beard. 'Real name's Pure Water, aye, but somebody called it Perdition because of the bad things that happen there. That's why it stuck.'

'Is that where you're headed?' Mav asked him.

'Got to go there,' Arnold said. 'Unfinished business,' he added with an air of mystery.

Mav didn't ask him what the

unfinished business was. Out in this semi-wilderness you kept your nose out of another man's business unless he forced the information down your throat.

'Strange town, Perdition,' Arnold reflected to himself.

'You mean halfway from pure to Hell?' Mav asked him.

Arnold gave a cackling laugh. 'Mostly Hell right down to the core,' he said. 'Founded by some kind of strange religious folk. Call themselves The Brotherhood. Then there's this sheriff, calls himself Bronco like I said.'

'Unlikely name for a man of the law,' Mav suggested as he rubbed Huckleberry's nose and spread the saddle blanket across his back.

'I didn't say he was a man of the law; I said he was the sheriff,' Arnold said. 'There's quite a difference as you must know.'

'I guess you mean he's part Hell?' Mav enquired.

'Bill Bronco is Hell itself,' Arnold

18

said. 'He's a giant and a bully. You must have heard of Bill Bronco in your travels?'

'Can't say I ever have,' Mav said. 'I don't read the papers much.'

Arnold spread his arms. 'Big as a mountain. Weighs in at around two hundred and twenty pounds. All muscle too. The kind of guy who will lay a man out in the dust with one blow. Fists like sledge hammers. Know what I mean?'

'Sounds like a man to avoid,' Mav said. 'Would he be part of your unfinished business by any chance?'

Arnold gave a broad grin. 'I just might have to kill him, that's all,' he admitted.

Mav understood completely. Perdition or Pure Water sounded like a contradiction but when a man has good intentions there was no problem. Maybe he should change his mind about riding in to Perdition and let Arnold ride in on his own.

*   *   *

Mav had a considerable curiosity. He reasoned that if you didn't look into things you never discovered anything. The idea of a sheriff who had been a heavyweight boxer fascinated him. So the two men rode into town around an hour later. Mav was struck by the clean lines and the purity of the place. There was dust, of course, but the sidewalks were swept clean and the façades of the buildings were mostly painted white and gleaming. Maybe it was Pure Water after all. As they rode down Main Street, Mav was acutely aware that they must have looked like two rather no-good saddle bums.

The sun was now shining bright in a cloudless sky and it was going to be a real scorcher of a day.

'Where are you headed?' Arnold asked, looking right and left down the deserted street.

'Nowhere in particular,' Mav said. 'Just somewhere to rest for a while, and maybe to find some kind of work, like I said, to keep me from going bankrupt.'

'You could try The Three Brothers,' Arnold advised. 'It's a place for good clean-living men with an inclination towards religion. I believe they sing psalms there on a Sunday so I wouldn't place a bet on it. When they see you coming they'll probably pull down the shutters and pretend to be having a prayer meeting.'

Mav cocked a humorous eye. 'I guess you don't sing too many psalms yourself. You mean the brothers, whoever they might be, are half-way to expecting you?'

'I have my own roosting place,' Arnold said. 'A more comfortable abode at the other end of town. You know what I mean?' He gave Mav a broad wink. He nodded towards what must have been the rather less salubrious end of town. 'See you then, partner.' He swung his flea-bitten nag into the middle of Main Street and rode on without turning his head.

Mav rubbed his chin and gave the matter some thought. He wasn't exactly soft, but he had his own standards which didn't include too much psalm singing.

He thought that maybe he should try The Three Brothers or even The Three Sisters, whoever they might be. While he was pondering on the matter, Arnold had already tied his horse to the hitching rail and had disappeared into a building further down Main Street. As Mav was pondering, he noticed a sign which said 'Sheriff's Office' and the next moment a big man appeared in the doorway.

Mav gave Huckleberry a little nudge with his spurs and the horse moved on towards the tower of muscle who must be Bill Bronco, the sheriff.

Bronco stood with his legs spread and his thumbs hooked into his belt. He was clean-shaven and impressive but Mav noticed he didn't carry a gun — maybe he figured he didn't need to.

'Morning,' Mav greeted in his most cheery tone. 'I guess you must be Sheriff Bill Bronco.'

Instead of replying, the sheriff cleared his throat and sent a stream of tobacco juice into the dust just beyond the side-walk. 'And who might you be, stranger?'

he growled in a muted baritone.

'Name's Mav,' Mav informed him politely. 'Thought I might find somewhere to rest up for a day or two. Catch my breath, so to speak. Maybe get a job.'

The sheriff squinted at him from the sidewalk and cleared his throat again. 'We don't go much on strangers at this end of town,' he said contemptuously. 'We're rather exclusive in that respect.'

'And I'm a little exclusive myself,' Mav retorted. 'So I guess I won't be hanging around for more than a day or two unless someone offers me the right employment.'

The sheriff squinted at him again and something seemed to click into place in his brain. 'Oh, we have a wise guy here, do we?' he said contemptuously.

Mav grinned at the big man. 'Just about average, I would say.'

The sheriff chewed a little more on his plug of tobacco. 'See you rode in with that no good skunk Jed Arnold,' he said.

'Just happened to meet him on the road,' Mav said.

'Did I hear you say your name is Mav?' the sheriff reflected. 'Mav what exactly?'

'Mav nothing,' Mav said. 'Just Mav. Everyone calls me Mav.'

The sheriff wasn't blessed with a great sense of humour and he looked distinctly unimpressed.

'That wouldn't be Mav alias Jesse Bolder who killed off the Big Bravo bunch in Cimarron a little while back, would it?' he enquired.

'That sounds like the same man,' Mav replied in a matter-of-fact tone. He wasn't the boastful type.

Bill Bronco was looking at him darkly from under the brim of a big black Stetson. He gave a brief sardonic nod. 'Well let me tell you something, Mr Mav,' he drawled. 'This is a peaceable town and we don't welcome killers around here.' Now he had a large hand spread on his chest like a patriot about to sing The Stars and Stripes for Ever.

'Fact is we pride ourselves on our peaceable nature in this town and I'm here to make that peace stand.' He leaned forward menacingly. 'I hope you heard what I just said.'

'Well, I did hear and I'd like to congratulate you on that,' Mav replied. 'I'm kinda fond of peace myself.'

No doubt more would have been said on both sides but there was a sudden intervention from further down Main Street where Jed Arnold had disappeared a few minutes before. It came in a series of sharp firecracker explosions followed by a much larger bang, followed by a waft of black smoke which came billowing out from one of the clapboard buildings.

'What the hell!' Bill Bronco exclaimed.

What the hell, indeed, thought Mav.

Though the sheriff was a big man he could move much more quickly than one might have expected. In less than a second he had disappeared into his office and reappeared strapping on his gun-belt.

'That Jed Arnold is running riot again!' he declared as he started at a jog towards the scene of the disturbance. It was, perhaps, more of a lumber than a jog but it served well enough.

Mav gigged Huckleberry forward with his spurs and they were on the scene of the disturbance in little more than a minute.

They weren't the only ones. A dilapidated buck-board was quickly on the scene, its crew bending and rising to pump water through a hose into the smoking building. And there was a wild mêlée in the street too. Half-naked women were screaming and men were knocking the daylights out of one another with their fists. Among them Mav recognized Jed Arnold, or what was left of him as he plunged backwards out of the bordello. He was shaking his bloody head and staggering around with blood streaming from his nose and one eye. He looked like a clown half made-up for a circus. Mav had never considered himself to be much of a pugilist but he did have a sense of loyalty. So he swung down from his horse and plunged straight in to drag Arnold out of the fray.

'Get out of here before you get yourself killed!' he shouted.

The women were screaming like harpies and one or two of the men were jeering and exchanging blows. That's all Mav remembered, because something like a giant hammer crashed into his face and, before he could clear his head, he was sprawling in the dust wondering how he got there. Next second he was out cold.

★   ★   ★

He came to and the jackhammer was still pounding relentlessly in his head. Where am I? he wondered, just as a pail of ice-cold water was flung over his face.

'How you doing?' a croaky old voice enquired.

Mav shook off the water and opened his eyes. Before him crouched a wizened old man who looked as though he had been whittled from the bark of an ancient pine tree. The old-timer was wheezing and laughing at the same time.

'Afraid you got in the way of a big fist there,' he said. 'Your eye's all right but he might have busted your jaw somewhat.'

Mav clutched at his jaw and worked it around a little. The sheriff's punch had obviously landed smack in the middle, knocking him right out cold. Otherwise he might have found it difficult to chew.

'You feeling hungry?' the old-timer asked him.

'Haven't had time to consider the matter yet,' Mav replied in a daze.

'Take your time,' the old-timer said.

Mav sat up cautiously and looked around. 'Why am I here in the hoosegow?' he asked.

The old-timer croaked. 'That's for the sheriff to decide,' he said. 'Sheriff Bronco has a very strict interpretation of the law around here.'

At that moment there was a groan from the next cell.

'That ain't nothing,' the old-timer explained. 'Just your partner complaining. He was hurt rather bad when the sheriff's fists connected with his jaw, especially since those fancy ladies had ripped him apart too. Lucky he wasn't shot down!'

Jed Arnold was still groaning in the next cell when the shadow of Bill Bronco fell across the entrance of Mav's cell. 'Like I told you,' the sheriff said. 'This is a peaceable town. We don't welcome troublemakers here. When I saw you and that no-good bum riding in to town together I knew I had no choice. That Jed Arnold is bad medicine in any town particularly here in Pure Water and we don't want him around.'

Mav was in no state to argue about that. His head was still thundering away like a whole bunch of rocks were bouncing around in it. He got up carefully from the horsehair mattress and swayed towards the door. Getting out into the air seemed a good idea.

The sheriff stood right in his way. 'If I let you out of this hoosegow you're going to ride out of town nice and easy and I don't want no more trouble. You understand what I'm saying to you?'

Mav stood with his hand against the door jamb. 'You're talking to the wrong man, Bronco. By my reckoning I just stopped by to pass the time of day with you. Next thing, your fist lams into my jaw and I'm in gaol. Is that the justice of Pure Water or Perdition? That's what I want to know.'

'What you want to know is your horse is at the hitching rail and you have to pay a fine and then hoof it out of town. That's what you want to know. By the way, I took the shells out of your guns in case you get some strange ideas into your head.'

Mav gave the sheriff a strange look and took his hat and shook the dust off it. He looked into the adjoining cell and saw Jed Arnold lying here, whining and groaning. One of his eyes was so black and swollen that he couldn't open it and his jaw was swathed in a blue bandanna. 'This *hombre* isn't fit to go anywhere. He needs a doctor,' Mav said.

The sheriff towered above him. 'Are you questioning my judgement?' he said. 'I say he's ready to hit the trail and you with him.' Then he made a big mistake. He laid a huge hand on Mav's shoulder as if to swivel him round and kick him through the door and on to the sidewalk.

Mav saw something like red flames soaring up in his head. Suddenly he remembered Big Bravo and the other gun-fighters he had had to kill back in Cimarron. Before he had time to consider, his reflexes took over. He had whipped around and jabbed Bill Bronco right in the gut where it hurts. Bronco might have been a prize-fighter way back and he might have been a giant but recently he had forgotten to do his press-ups and he was, to say the least, a little out of condition. When Mav's fist buried itself in his flesh he let out an involuntary gasp and jack-knifed forward.

Mav had a policy learned in the world of worldly wisdom. If you have to hit a man, hit him good and hard. If you step back and take a rest, he's going to come right at you like a raging bull and put you in hospital, maybe for ever. So, as the sheriff doubled up he brought up his knee and smashed it into his face. Bill Bronco lurched back with surprising speed and he might have collapsed on the floor, but Mav hadn't finished yet. He pulled the sheriff up by the ears and bounced his head on the wall a couple of times and then once more for luck. The sheriff stared at him in horror and disbelief for half a second. Then he slid down the wall and fell unconscious on to the floor.

'My gawd, you killed sheriff!' the old-timer whined. 'You killed sheriff Bronco! How'd you do that?'

'Self-defence,' Mav reminded him. 'A matter of self-defence. And I think he'll live, anyway.' He turned towards the old-timer. 'Now you just get those keys and open up this other cell and that's all we need apart from our weaponry.'

'Yes sir, yes sir.' The old man scooted over to the key rack, took down the appropriate key and unlocked Jed Arnold's cell. 'Well I'll be damned,' he said. 'I ain't never seen nothing like that afore.'

'And I hope you don't see anything like that again,' Mav said as he strapped on his gun-belt and checked his shooter.

Jed Arnold had rolled out of his bunk, staggered to his feet and got out of his cell with admirable speed considering his state of health. 'Well, dang me,' he said. 'A man sees a miracle every dog-gone day!' Though he looked a mess and no doubt should have been in hospital, he didn't want to hang around any longer than he needed to.

As Mav helped him through the door, he got a surprise. Half the town of Perdition seemed to be standing there, looking past them in amazement.

'My gawd, you killed the sheriff!' a

smart looking dude exclaimed without too much regret.

'Not quite,' Mav replied, 'I think you'll find he'll live a little bit longer.' He glanced back over his shoulder and saw that the sheriff was still hunched up in the corner and breathing like a buffalo that had been hit by an avalanche of boulders. The old-timer was staring down at his convulsed visage as though he couldn't believe his eyes.

'You'd better get out of town pronto,' the man in the dark suit advised. 'Sheriff Bronco has a mean streak and he'll be wanting to get even with you as soon as he's on his feet again.'

'That's his problem,' Mav growled. 'I aim to stick around for a while. Rest up for a few days. Get my strength back.'

'You don't know how ornery that man can be,' the smart dude warned him again.

'I think I caught a glimpse of that,' Mav said. 'Can you point me in the direction of The Three Brothers?'

'Well, The Three Brothers is back

there a piece.' The dude pointed off to the right.

'Thank you for your directions.' Mav mounted Huckleberry and gave the horse a comforting word. 'Don't you worry too much, old buddy,' he said. 'There's plenty of storms in a tea cup and that was just one of them.'

Jed Arnold was still only half-conscious and he had to be helped into the saddle by several reluctant hands.

'If you don't mind me asking, where are you going?' Mav asked him. 'Looks like you need the quack to look at those wounds of yours.'

'Well, you don't look too great yourself,' Arnold mumbled somewhat ungraciously. 'Did I hear you mention The Three Brothers?'

Mav wasn't altogether delighted to have Jed Arnold riding along with him. 'You don't seem to be too popular in this crazy town,' he said. 'What's with you, anyway?'

'A man is known here,' Arnold admitted with his head hanging down over his horse's neck. 'Like I told you, unfinished business.'

'Some business. First few minutes you step into town a swarm of floozies starts tearing your limbs apart, a house goes up in flames and you nearly get yourself killed by flying lead. That sounds like bad business to me,' Mav said. 'Gives an associate an evil reputation.'

They were now outside a large building with the legend 'The Three Brothers' painted above it in blue and gold lettering. 'Looks like a nice respectable kind of establishment,' Mav said as he dismounted and tethered Huckleberry to the hitching rail. 'Now you just rest up for a moment or two,' he said to the horse. 'I'm going in here to make a few enquiries. Then we'll find you a good place to rest up. You hear me?'

Huckleberry tossed his head and snickered.

'You staying there on your horse or what?' Mav said to Arnold.

Arnold made no audible reply. His head had sunk down low on the saddle and he seemed to be far away in fairyland.

Mav climbed the step and went in through the door of The Three Brothers. He went over to reception and rang a bell, but there was no immediate response. He rang the bell again and waited. Somewhere out in the back he thought he heard furtive movements but still nobody came. When he turned towards the door again he saw a figure in a dark suit standing there like the statue of doom.

'You won't get any service here,' the man said and Mav recognized him as the dude who had given him directions outside the caboose.

'That so?' Mav jangled the bell again.

The dude took a breath. 'I think I warned you,' he said. 'Sheriff Bronco is all fired up and he'll be coming to get you. He wears two guns, cross draw and he looks in a very ugly mood.'

'Must be a little winded,' Mav said.

'Maybe he should go back into his corner and rest a while.'

'This is no laughing matter,' said the dude. 'When Bronco's humiliated he gets real mean. There are half a dozen men lying up there on Boot Hill who thought they could get the better of Bronco and they didn't die of bruised jaws either.'

'Sounds like a real law-abiding sheriff you got here.'

'Well, we don't want the whole place broken up, do we?' the dude said.

Mav went over to the window and squinted between the curtains. Jed Arnold and his horse were nowhere to be seen but he saw the ex-boxer Bill Bronco making his way at a very determined but unsteady gait towards The Three Brothers. As the dude had said he wore two gun-belts cross draw and he was nursing a Winchester carbine in his left arm.

'You weren't exaggerating, mister,' Mav said. 'And thanks for the warning.'

'Don't mention it,' said the the dude

38

in the black suit. 'Maybe you should step outside and face the music or disappear through the back entrance. This is a respectable establishment and we don't want trouble here.'

'Thanks again,' Mav said. 'In that case, I think it has to be the music. By the way, I don't think I caught your name.'

'That's because I didn't throw it,' the man said. 'I'm Obediah Bead and I'm one of the brothers mentioned on the sign. And, by the way, we have no vacancies.' He turned and disappeared abruptly behind a curtain that led to an office and presumably to an escape route through a back door.

Mav parted the curtains and looked out again. Bill Bronco was now standing close to the hitching rail and looking up at The Three Brothers. He was swaying slightly and breathing hard and he shook his head to drive away the cobwebs in his brain. He then shifted the Winchester into a more comfortable position with his right hand close to the trigger. To his right and left were several other men formed up like a posse and they were also carrying Winchesters.

Mav adjusted his gun-belt and stepped out on to the sidewalk.

*   *   *

As soon as Mav saw the expression in Bronco's eyes he knew he had a problem on his hands. Injured pride has killed many a man and Bronco's pride had been injured in a really big way, as those graves on Boot Hill testified.

'You looking for someone?' Mav asked the big man. That was an unfortunate opening. Several of Bronco's buddies were grinning and one of them gave a low chuckle. The chuckle didn't do much to soothe Bronco's pride and, as he turned his head to quieten the man, Mav drew his Colt in a quick and easy motion.

When Bronco's eyes returned to Mav, he saw Mav standing with the barrel of the Colt lying across his left arm. Bronco's buddies had drawn back slightly as though suddenly realizing that something serious and deadly might be about to occur and they were in the line of fire.

'Well.' Mav spoke quietly but directly. 'I'm always ready to talk, Sheriff Bronco. I think it's best to talk a little. If men stop talking there's liable to be a lot of blood spilled all over the sidewalk — and that could make a mess in a nice town like this, couldn't it?'

That caused a flutter among Bronco's *brave* supporters. Maybe some of them had heard how Mav had gunned down the Big Bravo Gang close to Cimarron and reputations can become exaggerated when tongues begin to wag. Maybe this man who called himself Mav had shot down as many as twenty men like William Bonney, alias Billy the Kid!

Bronco paused to consider matters and Mav knew he had to do something to relieve the tension.

'Tell you something, Sheriff,' he said.

'You want peace in this town, I want peace in this town. No sense in spoiling its reputation, is there?'

Bronco moved his feet and swayed forward slightly. 'Like I told you, you leave town like I said. Either you ride out peaceably or you go out dead. It's your decision.'

Mav grinned. 'Sure I'm leaving town,' he replied laconically. 'Just as soon as I'm good and ready.'

Bronco tightened his lip and his henchmen braced themselves for the coming confrontation. 'I tell you you're moving out right now,' he challenged. 'That is unless you want to spend a week or two in jail and come up before the judge for assaulting an officer of the law.'

Mav paused. 'Tell you something, Sheriff. Nobody wants anyone to get hurt around here. Why don't we do this good and legal?'

'What's that supposed to mean?' Bronco asked, obviously somewhat perplexed.

'What it means,' Mav said, 'is we fight it out in the ring, bare-knuckled, man to man.'

A look of total bafflement appeared on the sheriffs face. Then he gave a hoarse laugh of incredulity. 'You mean you and me in the ring?' he said a semitone higher.

'Better than blowing holes in our heads with bullets,' Mav suggested.

There was a moment of silent astonishment. Then a ripple of laughter ran through the posse members: 'This man must be right off his head!' 'He wants to commit suicide!' 'Doesn't he care for his own hide?' The tension had eased and everyone began laughing and one or two members of the posse threw their hats in the air and started taking bets.

Mav saw that Bronco was laughing too in a somewhat harsh and derisory tone. 'OK,' Bronco said. 'I'll take you up on that, cowboy. You can have a week or two to get your muscles good and hard. Then we'll fix it up. I'll squash you like a dead fly! That's what I'll do.'

He turned away laughing and returned with his bunch to the sheriff's office.

3

'That was a pretty damned foolhardy thing to do,' someone said from close beside Mav. Mav turned to see Obediah Bead standing three feet away from him.

'You think so?' he said.

Bead shook his head slowly as though he pitied Mav. 'You ever been in the ring with a prize-fighter half as heavy again as yourself?' Bead marvelled.

'Don't think I ever have,' Mav reflected.

'Why did you make that nonsensical challenge?' Bead asked in amazement.

Mav holstered his Colt. 'Seemed like a good idea at the time,' he said. 'Better than shooting a man full of holes. I don't like the look of blood spurting from a man's body especially on the sidewalk outside a respectable establishment like this. Makes me feel sick to my stomach.'

'Well, Bronco won't forget that,' Bead said. 'He'll punch the daylights out of you when you meet him in the ring. You do know that, don't you?'

'Sure.' Mav nodded. 'We'll take care of that when the time comes.' He was looking at Bead closely. He saw a man of around five ten with a dark moustache and rather intent eyes; a man who was somewhat particular about the way he dressed; a man who was no longer hostile towards him; a man with an obvious sense of humour.

'You got a couple of weeks,' Bead said. 'What do you aim to do?'

Mav shrugged. 'Find some place to stay,' he replied. 'Wash up, feed up, and build up my strength.'

'What about your partner, Jed Arnold?' Bead asked.

'He's no partner of mine. I've never seen him before yesterday. We just happened to ride in together. I guess he's gone to ask the quack to patch him up a little. He doesn't look too healthy at the moment.'

Bead looked thoughtful. 'Tell you what,' he said. 'You got a couple of weeks maybe before your death sentence. Why don't you stay here at The Three Brothers? We could give you a reasonable deal. My wife's a fine cook. You need feeding up if you're going to stand any chance with that prize-fighter.'

Mav grinned. 'I thought you said you had no vacancies.'

Bead chuckled quietly. 'A man can change his mind, you know. I liked the cool way you dealt with Bronco. A bit like a good poker game. Do you play poker, five card draw, any of that stuff?'

Mav shook his head. 'Never had time for any of that. Too busy living,' he said.

'Well, then,' Bead chuckled. 'You can stay here like a turkey being fattened up for Christmas. How would that be?'

Mav considered. 'I don't care for the comparison,' he said. 'But what's the executioner going to think about that?'

'We have to take a chance on that,' Bead said. 'My guess is that Bronco will be taking bets on you going down in the first round, maybe even in the first second. So he aims to get rich. He might even think of you as his prize turkey, at that. So why don't you just come inside and set yourself down?'

'What about my horse, Huckleberry?'

'Take your horse to the livery just a step down the street. Then go to Doc Blandish and ask him to take a look at your bruises. You look a bit beat up already and we want our turkey to be in prime condition, don't we?'

*   *   *

Doc Blandish had given up serious medicine some years before but he was still quite good at patching people up. Some said he wasn't a real doctor but had qualified as a dentist like the so-called Doc Halliday. When Mav arrived he was examining Jed Arnold and feeling around to see whether he had any broken bones.

'Tell you something,' he said with a

southern drawl. 'You're lucky your jaw's not broken and you're gonna keep the sight of that eye. I've seen a man die within a week after an encounter with Bill Bronco. That sheriff is more than a bully; he's a damned murderer. Somebody should run him out of town before he does any more damage.'

That was ominous.

'Sounds like he's not so popular in this town,' Mav suggested.

Doc Blandish shook his head. 'Just about as popular as a rattlesnake,' he said. 'Too many bad things have happened around here since he took the badge of office and it went right to his head. The good people want to be rid of him but it isn't so easy to dethrone a tyrant. That's a well known fact. Take those Tsars in Russia. I hear you challenged Bronco to a fist fight. That was a damned fool thing to do.'

'Better than blowing a hole in his head,' Mav speculated.

'You go ahead with this fist fight, he might end up putting you up on Boot

Hill like the rest of them,' the doctor said.

Doc Blandish was attending to Jed Arnold's wounds. 'I believe I know you, don't I?' he said.

'I think you might,' Arnold admitted.

'I understand you were caught up in a brawl in the cat house down there. That's right,' he reflected. 'A man broke a bottle over your head and I had to patch you up a while back.'

'You did a good job,' Arnold said. 'I got the scars to prove it.' He pointed to a livid scar above his right ear.

'So you were foolish enough to come back,' the doctor said. 'May I ask why?'

Arnold winced. 'Unfinished business,' he said.

'You can't be staying at The Three Brothers, can you?' the doctor asked him.

Arnold gave a prolonged chuckle and winced again. 'They don't take bums like me at The Three Brothers. I'm not high-faluting enough. So I stay at Madam Maisie's place. Anyways, I got friends down there and business too.'

'Like I said — the cat house,' the Doc remarked dryly. 'I heard the place took fire down there as soon as you arrived and all those floozies came out and set upon you,' the Doc said.

'Just a little welcoming party,' Arnold replied. 'Some fool just threw a pan of flaming oil in my direction. That's what started the fire. And those women were just greeting me. That's the way they show respect for a man here in 'Perdition'. If that sheriff hadn't butted in with his clumsy fists everything would have been hunky-dory.' He turned to Mav 'I could have put in a good word for you too, saved you from that tight arsed place down there.'

'At least you get a bit of peace and quiet down at The Three Brothers,' Mav said.

Arnold gave his throaty chuckle. 'Well, see you later, partner.'

He mounted his flea-bitten horse and rode away to the darker side of town.

Mav wasn't sorry to be rid of Jed Arnold who, he figured, was bad luck to anyone. He went back to The Three Brothers and took a long hot bath. Then he spruced himself up, had a proper shave, and went down to the room with the soft chairs and sank down to luxuriate. The Three Brothers felt more like Heaven than Perdition.

There were three other people in the room, a woman and two men. One of the men looked like a sewing-machine salesman. The other had a long grey beard and was studying a black book that looked like the Bible. The woman was a large lady with her face turned away from Mav. She looked vaguely familiar but Mav couldn't for the moment recall where he'd seen her before.

As Mav was looking in her direction and trying to remember, the man with the long grey beard turned slowly to look at him. 'Well, young man,' he growled, 'and what brings you to town?'

'Just minding my own business,' Mav replied.

The Bible reader who must have been around sixty nodded approvingly. 'Quite so,' he said. 'I had no right to ask.' He leaned forward with a look of enquiry. 'May I say, sir, that what you did out there was thoroughly admirable. I was watching from a distance and I was deeply impressed.'

Mav regarded him warily but the old man was nodding and smiling quite benignly. 'I had thought of intervening, young man, but as you see I'm a little long in the tooth and something of a coward. I thought you handled the situation with admirable wisdom though I don't envy you when it comes to bare-fisted boxing.' He stretched out a long-fingered, sensitive-looking hand. 'The Reverend Montague Means,' he said.

Mav took the rather limp fingers and gave them a squeeze. The other man and the woman were now studying him inquisitively.

'But I have to ask you,' the Reverend Montague Means continued. 'How do you intend to extricate yourself when it is time to meet the challenge? I take it you're a pugilist yourself?'

Mav wasn't sure about the word pugilist. Was it some kind of snake or a Japanese wrestler, he wondered.

'I think we'll let that take care of itself,' he said. 'What happens is what happens.'

'Admirably philosophical,' the preacher said. 'Though it might be a good idea to have some sort of plan in mind.'

'What kind of plan would that be?' Mav asked.

The preacher raised his eyebrows and grinned under his copious beard. 'You could always throw a fit or something or just ride out of town. Some would sneak in and put a tranquilliser in the man's drink.'

'I'm looking at all possibilities,' Mav said.

He didn't want to listen to any more preaching, so he turned his attention to the woman who was now looking directly into his eyes. As he met her gaze she was already halfway to her feet. She was a tall woman and he suddenly knew who she was.

'Brassy Baby!' he exclaimed. 'What brings you here?'

A look of surprise and embarrassment appeared in her eyes. 'I'm not Brassy Baby any more,' she whispered. 'You got the wrong woman.' Now she was smiling again. 'I'm Queenie Caryl, the actress, now. That's how I'm known.'

'Well, Queenie, it's good to meet you again.' Of course he remembered all that had happened in Cimarron those few years ago, how he had had to kill Big Bravo and Coyote Ben and the others, and how he had lodged with Gladness, and how Gladness and Brassy Baby had decided to throw in with Sadie Solomon and Joe Basnett and try their hand in their acting group after the big showdown.

He still remembered how Gladness

had turned and waved goodbye to him as the Butterfield stage pulled out. It was a strange and haunting memory that was still shining brightly in his mind.

'How is Gladness?' he asked.

'Oh, Gladness is doing real well,' Queenie said. 'She's right along with the rest of us. She has a voice like a lovebird. We're hoping to do a show here in Pure Water. That's why I'm here to talk to Mr Obediah Bead.'

The Reverend Montague Means had listened to all this with some interest. He had closed his Bible and was leaning forward with intent. 'Did I hear you talking about theatricals, my good lady?' he enquired.

Queenie turned to him with one of her most alluring smiles. 'Yes, you did,' she said. 'I represent the Sadie Solomon's Theatre Company. We're doing a show in a barn just outside town. The MacKinleys' place. I hope you'll come along Reverend and enjoy.'

The Reverend Montague Means nodded

sagely. 'I don't think I can manage to come to your *performance*, dear lady. As a man of the cloth I don't approve of theatricals and such frivolities.' However, he was still smiling benignly: Queenie Caryl was still a very handsome woman, though perhaps a little faded.

'Well, I hope you change your mind,' she said.

★　★　★

As Obediah Bead had promised, his wife, a short dumpy woman, turned out to be an excellent cook. Presently Mav found himself sitting at a polished oak table tucking into goose stew with dumplings and as many trimmings as were available in this territory. On his left, at the head of the table, sat the Reverend Montague Means and on his right sat the apparently closed-mouthed sewing-machine salesman. Opposite him, Obediah Bead was studying him closely.

'So you're one of the brothers,' Mav said. 'Where are the other two?'

Bead smiled from under his dark moustache. 'I had two brothers,' he admitted. 'My brother Peter pulled out and went to California to found a mission there. My younger brother Joe was killed by a gunman at Stinking Ridge about two miles from here. We were never quite sure who it was who killed him or why it happened.'

'I'm sorry to hear that,' Mav said.

'We wanted the place to be honest and good,' Bead said. 'That was why we founded The Three Brothers.'

'Alleluia!' said the preacher.

'Is that why you elected Bill Bronco sheriff?' Mav asked with irony.

Obediah Bead and the Reverend Montague Mean exchanged uneasy glances. 'That was a bad mistake,' Bead admitted. 'We thought he would keep the peace but he has stirred up a deal of trouble.'

'He has that,' agreed the Reverend. 'Half of Boot Hill is devoted to his victims.'

The sewing-machine salesman looked

up suddenly and spoke. 'Those actor friends of yours will never get permission to do their plays,' he said in a sepulchral tone. 'I heard Bronco talking the other day. He's going to run them right out of town.' His eyes darted round in alarm. 'Please don't quote me on that. I'm hoping to do some business here.'

The Reverend Montague Means was studying Mav with shrewd beady eyes. 'If you want my advice, my good sir,' he said. 'I would say instead of indulging in fisticuffs with Bill Bronco you should ride down to the MacKinleys' place while your hide is still intact and advise your actor friends to get right out of town and you should go with them too for your own health. That's my considered opinion.'

Mav took up the napkin Mrs Bead had so thoughtfully provided and wiped his mouth clean. 'Well, thank you for that,' he said. 'I'll take a look at your advice from all angles.' He got up from the table and put the napkin down in its place. 'In the meantime,' he said, 'I think I've got a hankering to greet my old friends down at the MacKinley place, anyway.'

He turned at the door and nodded. The men at the table were looking at him in wonder and dread, but Obediah Bead seemed to be smiling secretly under his black moustache.

* * *

He took his time riding to the MacKinley spread which was just a short distance beyond the edge of town. He was trying to work things out in his mind and he had a few words with Huckleberry on the way.

'Point is, Huck, do I stay or do I leave like the Reverend said?'

Huckleberry tossed his head.

'Sure. I know,' Mav agreed. 'You pull out of town, you avoid a heap of trouble. You remember what happened back in Cimarron. If I had kept a little quieter I could have avoided being almost shot to pieces there.'

Huckleberry jogged along quite happily.

'Yes, you're right at that,' Mav agreed. 'If I hadn't ridden into Cimarron that day I wouldn't have met Gladness either, would I?'

'No you wouldn't,' Huckleberry seemed to agree with a shake of his head.

'What's with Gladness, anyway?' Mav remarked to himself. 'She's just the good woman I lodged with one time. And when I rode out of Cimarron after all that nonsense we thought we were saying goodbye for ever.' Nevertheless, he still remembered that frail white hand waving to him as the Butterfield stage pulled out.

Now he came to an arch with a pair of buffalo horns above it. Underneath, painted somewhat crudely, was the legend 'MacKinley Horse Ranch'. As he turned in at the entrance he saw a modest sized house of timber and, close by, a wagon. Beside the wagon several people were sitting at a trestle table eating their supper. Three of them were women and one was a man. He recognized them all immediately. There was Queenie Caryl, of course, and Sadie Solomon, and Joe Basnett. Above all there was Gladness herself. She was the first to see him. She pushed aside her plate and ran to meet him.

'Mr Mav!' she said. 'How good to see you!'

It was more than good. It was a miracle. Mav dismounted to meet her. He couldn't make up his mind whether to shake her hand or kiss her on the cheek, but, before he could decide, she had wrapped her arms around him and their lips had decided for them.

'You've been fighting,' she said, drawing back in dismay.

'Not exactly fighting,' he said modestly. 'I just collided with the sheriff's fist, that's all.'

She took him by the hand. 'Come and sit with us,' she said. 'Tell me some of the good things that have happened to you.'

This was Gladness. Not the sad Gladness he had known in Cimarron, but a newly restored Gladness with a smile and an open heart.

'Looks like the acting profession really agrees with you,' he said.

Sadie Solomon, a dark and slightly overblown woman wearing an Apache shawl over her shoulders, gave a loud hoot of laughter. 'I've been real lucky,' she said. 'Queenie and Gladness have a deal of talent between them. Joe here does the writing and I do the managing and directing. You'll be surprised when you hear Gladness do her act. She can sing like a bird, sometimes high and sometimes low. Sometimes joyful and sometimes sad. Funny how the public likes a good cry.'

Under this avalanche of praise Gladness reddened slightly and avoided Mav's eye. Joe Basnett was smiling modestly too. He was probably thinking of the time the Comanches rescued him from death and brought him back to Cimarron.

'You think they'll let us do our show?'

he asked quietly.

'No question,' Mav said. 'If the people want your show, you can put it on. There's nobody can stop you.'

That gave rise to a faint murmur of approval in which Sam MacKinley and his wife Sarah had joined. They had just emerged from the ranch house with their two children, a boy and a girl of six or seven. The MacKinleys were both tall and raw-boned frontier people. Nobody had ever told MacKinley what to do. He stepped forward and crushed Mav's hand between his hard boney fingers. 'Heard about you,' he said, 'how you killed that criminal bunch in Cimarron.'

'Well, that was just one of those things that happen,' Mav said modestly.

'See you still wear your shooter,' the rancher said.

'Matter of habit,' Mav told him. 'Without it on my hip I'd think I'd left my pants at home.'

That provoked another round of laughter.

Before anything more could be said there was the sound of a horse approaching at speed and one of MacKinley's hands came galloping under the buffalo horns towards them. He reined in beside them. 'There's trouble in town!' the man shouted.

'What trouble?' Sam MacKinley demanded.

'Big trouble the other end of town,' the man blustered. 'A real bad shoot out! Down near Maisie's place. Something to do with a man called Jed Arnold who rode in this morning. They say men are being killed down there.'

* * *

Jed Arnold doesn't mean anything to me, Mav thought as he mounted up. Am I a nursemaid or something? Nevertheless, he ignored the pleas that came at him from round the trestle table and from the MacKinleys themselves.

'Don't go looking for trouble!' Sam

MacKinley said.

'Keep yourself out of this!' Queenie shouted hoarsely.

None of those shouts meant anything to him. The only thing that concerned him was Gladness's look of alarm as he turned to glance at her. Suddenly he remembered how her husband and her two children had been massacred by the Apache Indians all those years before and the terrible way she had looked when she told him the story.

Mav never liked to hurry. A man who hurries can get himself shot before he knows what's hit him. So he just rode on steadily right past the livery stable and The Three Brothers, and on towards the part of town where Jed Arnold had disappeared earlier. *Unfinished business,* Mav thought, what kind of unfinished business? And what had he to do with Jed Arnold, the man who had intended to rob him the night before?

As he approached the other end of town, he saw a sizeable crowd stretched half-way across the street, among them Obediah Bead and the Reverend Montague Means. The Reverend still had his Bible in his hand. In fact he was chanting something from it in a clear and solemn tone.

'I could have foretold it,' Obediah Bead said as Mav dismounted. 'I saw death written in every crease of that man's face.'

Mav tethered Huckleberry to the hitching rail and pushed his way through the crowd to where Doc Blandish was bending over the form of a man. As Mav approached the doc looked back over his shoulder. 'Not much I can do, I fear,' he said. 'To think I patched him up no more than three hours past and look at him now.'

Mav got down on one knee and leaned forward. The man lying with his back in the dust of the street was Jed Arnold. He had three bullet holes, one in his left arm and two in his chest, just above the heart. There was a great deal of blood on his ripped shirt and on his beard. But he was still conscious.

He raised his head slightly and a look of recognition flickered in his eyes. 'Is that you, partner?' he said.

'This is Mav,' Mav said.

Arnold gave a twisted distortion of a grin. 'Funny name, Mav,' he said faintly. Then he coughed and blood came spurting from his mouth.

'Easy there,' the doc soothed. 'Easy there. Rest back and lie.'

Now the Reverend Montague Means was close, half-bowing towards the dying man. He was chanting something from one of the psalms: 'The Lord is my Shepherd . . . '

'Listen, buddy,' Arnold gasped. 'There's something I got to say to you.' He reached out for Mav's hand.

Mav waited as Doc Blandish cradled the man's head. 'Take it easy,' he soothed.

'I want you to have it . . . ' Arnold slurred.

'Want him to have what?' Doc Blandish asked him.

'I want . . . I want . . . ' Arnold was

trying to gather himself together for one last effort, but it was too late. There was a rattle in his throat and then a long sigh.

'Dead,' pronounced the doc prosaically.

'You know what he was trying to say to you?' the Reverend Montague Means asked Mav.

'I have no idea,' Mav said.

But his mind was on other things.

4

Doc Blandish closed Jed Arnold's vacant eyes and Mav stood up and looked around. Another man lay crumpled up and dead on the sidewalk a few paces away. A number of women with heavily painted faces were staring around in dismay with their fists stuffed into their mouths. And Sheriff Bronco was standing some distance away surveying the scene like a king looking over his kingdom. He still had his Frontier Colt in his hand.

Jed Arnold no longer had his gun. It was cast away as much as a yard from his hand. Mav stooped and retrieved it and found that all six chambers had been discharged. He walked over to the body lying on the sidewalk and looked down at the man's glazed eyes. 'Who's this?' he asked one of the grieving women.

The woman was in too much of a panic to reply. She burst into tears and disappeared into the bordello. Another bolder woman sidled up to Mav. 'They were talking in there. There was a brawl and it spilled out here.'

Mav turned and saw Bill Bronco advancing with his gun hanging by his side. 'Pity about your friend,' he said with a sneer. 'He was dead set on getting himself killed. That's the way it was.' He shrugged and nodded complacently.

'That's the way it was,' Mav repeated. 'Who shot Arnold?' he asked the sheriff.

'Might have been this dumb critter,' Bronco said, pointing his Colt at the dead man.

'Then again it might have been you,' Mav suggested with his eye on the trailing Colt.

'And it might have been me,' the sheriff gloated. 'Like I said, this is a law abiding town and I aim to keep it that way.'

'Arnold had three bullet holes, one in his left arm and two in his chest,' Mav said. 'His gun was thrown down like he was trying to give himself up. How do you read that, Sheriff?'

The big man gave a self-satisfied smirk. 'I read it like it was,' he said. 'After Arnold shot this man lying here dead on the ground, he turned his gun on me and I had to shoot him in self-defence.'

'Three shots and two of them fatal,' Mav said, 'and it looks like he had thrown his gun down already.'

Bill Bronco was measuring Mav with his eye. 'Are you accusing me of murder, cowboy?' he asked aggressively.

Mav glanced down at Bronco's gun and saw that he already had his trigger finger under the trigger guard. The sheriff could raise that single-action Colt and fire it point blank into Mav's chest before he had time to breathe or draw. Mav knew he might do it but he refused to flinch or back off. 'I'm just looking at the facts here,' he said.

Most of the crowd were still standing around looking at the bodies but a few were now close to Mav and the sheriff — but not too close in case they got hit by a stray bullet. Bronco was obviously used to the limelight because of his earlier boxing career. 'These men are scum, anyway,' he said. 'They don't deserve to live in a peaceable community like Pure Water.'

There was a murmur from close by. Mav noticed from the corner of his eye that the Reverend Montague Means was stroking his beard and he still had his Bible held defensively close to his chest. A little further off Obediah Bead was looking somewhat anxiously in Mav's direction. A man in a black suit and his young assistant were already lifting Jed Arnold's body and lowering it into a coffin.

'Arnold was not scum,' Mav said. 'He was just a saddle bum and he deserved a better end than you gave him.'

'Listen, cowboy.' Bronco advanced a step so that he was looking right down at Mav from his full six foot four. He was now too close to Mav to use his

Colt, but still Mav refused to budge. 'Listen, cowboy,' Bronco repeated, 'you may think you're a hero but to me you're nothing more than a bum like that no-good partner of yours lying there dead. You brought trouble to this town and I won't rest until you ride right out again, on your horse or feet first, whichever you prefer. It makes no nevermind to me.'

He shrugged again and turned away. For a moment Mav could have drawn his gun and shot him in his exposed back. But that wasn't Mav's way.

'By the way.' Bronco swung round again. 'I'm looking forward to meeting you in the ring, that's if you survive long enough.' He leaned forward and stuck out his prominent jaw. 'You know what, Mr Mav, I'm going to punch you all round that ring and leave you so your mother wouldn't recognize you.'

Mav's face suddenly broke out in a grin. 'I shall look forward to that,' he said.

Instead of returning to The Three Brothers, Mav mounted the sidewalk and went in through the doors of the bordello. He wasn't sure why but he knew in the back of his mind that there was some reason and it had to to with Jed Arnold's last words: *I want you to have it.*

As he stood in the entrance, looking round and catching the stale scent that wafted around, he also thought of Bronco's last words: *I'm going to punch you all round that ring and leave you so your mother wouldn't recognize you.* And he could do it too, Mav thought fatalistically.

Now as he stood waiting, a woman who looked as though she was made up for a circus act came out and confronted him. 'What do you want?' she bawled with her hands on her broad hips. 'We don't want no more trouble around here. There's two men dead and another bleeding in here. I know you're a buddy of that man Arnold and I don't want you nosing around here. So you'd better get out right away.'

'To begin with, Arnold and me were not buddies,' Mav replied. 'We just happened to ride in together. He's dead now, so maybe you could show some respect.'

'Then, why are you here?' she asked, blocking his way. 'You come to do business? This is no time for business. When a man dies trade drops off sudden like.'

'I just want to look see where Arnold was set to stay. I think there might be something for me in there.'

'That's most unlikely,' she said hotly. 'If you weren't his buddy, how come he would have anything for you?'

'That's what I'm here to find out,' Mav said.

'OK.' She moved sideways to let him pass. 'I'll show you where he was set to stay and then you must go before the sheriff comes in after you. I don't want no trouble in here. This is a respectable house.'

On the way up the rickety stairs they came to an open door through which Mav caught sight of Doc Blandish tending the man who was bleeding. Doc Blandish paused to glance in Mav's direction. 'What are you doing here?' he asked anxiously.

'I'm not sure,' Mav replied. 'Just a hunch, I guess.'

'Your hunches are going to get you killed if you don't watch yourself,' the doc said. 'If the sheriff saw you coming in here he might try to arrest you. And we don't want any more gunplay today, do we?'

Mav made no reply. He was looking past the doc at the man lying on the bed who had a wound in the shoulder which Doc Blandish had been doing his best to stanch.

'Who shot you?' Mav asked him.

Though the man grimaced with pain he was able to talk. 'Arnold and me had a difference of opinion about a woman,' he said hoarsely. 'It's long standing. Arnold gunned down on me. That's how the whole thing started. Shot me clean through the shoulder.'

'Just about a woman,' Mav said.

'Is there anything else?' the wounded man muttered between his teeth.

'Get along,' the woman with the clown's face urged.

Mav went on to the floor above.

'This is where he lodged,' the woman said, throwing the door open.

Mav went in bending low so as not to collide with the ceiling beams. The room was small and cramped, little more than a cupboard. Mav recognized Arnold's bundle lying on the floor close to the unmade bed. *I want you to have it,* Mav thought as he stood on the threshold. Have what? he wondered.

'You want to take his bundle, you're welcome,' the woman said.

Mav reached into the bundle and found a wallet. Maybe Arnold wanted him to have that. Mav looked inside and saw a fat wad of dollars, more than he would have expected a saddle bum like Arnold to carry.

'Are those greenbacks?' the woman asked. 'If they are they belong to me.'

Mav peeled off a few of the bills and held them out. 'There's enough here to pay for his room ten times over,' he said.

'What about the rest?' she asked suspiciously.

'The rest goes with me,' Mav said. He was looking at a mysterious package hidden away in the corner of the wallet. 'They'll help towards the funeral expenses.'

'I don't think the sheriff would like to hear about that,' she threatened.

Mav stowed the wallet away in the inner pocket of his vest. 'Sheriff Bronco is no friend of yours. After this incident he's more than likely to close you down.' He picked up Arnold's pathetic bundle and hefted it on to his shoulder.

When he stepped out on to the sidewalk, the undertaker and his assistant were loading two coffins on to a buckboard. The crowd was still gaping around as if they were waiting for some kind of sequel. The sheriff was still standing in the middle of Main Street like a king. The only person to approach Mav was Obediah Bead.

'So you went to that den of iniquity,' he said to Mav.

'No law against going into a building, especially in broad daylight,' Mav replied. 'I had to collect Arnold's worldly goods.'

Bead looked thoughtful. 'You don't bring much into the world,' he said, 'and you don't take much out when you leave it.' He eyed the pathetic bundle.

'Let that be a lesson to us all,' Mav replied. 'Especially that murderous sheriff of yours. I'm going on down to the livery stable to pick up Arnold's pathetic nag.'

Now it was getting towards sundown and well nigh time for Mav to hit the hay. As he rode down to The Three Brothers, he passed Sheriff Bronco who was standing with his thumbs hooked into his gun-belts.

'See you got your reward,' Bronco mocked.

Mav swung the bundle on to his shoulder. 'It might not be much but it'll have to do,' he said as he rode on to the livery stable.

* * *

The old geek who ran the livery stable was feeding the horses. When he saw Mav coming he stiffened as though expecting trouble.

'I guess you've come to ask me to put that poor old critter down,' he said in a whining voice.

'If you're talking about Jed Arnold's horse, don't bother,' Mav said. 'Every creature needs a good home. If he's too old to work, he needs to be put out to grass.' Mav looked at Arnold's horse and examined its teeth. 'How much did Arnold owe you?' he enquired.

The old geek, whose rheumy eyes brightened at the mention of money, named a price.

'That's steep,' Mav said, peeling off a few more dollars from Arnold's wallet.

'Take good care of these too horses until tomorrow and I'll let you know.'

'You leaving town?' the old geek enquired.

'I don't think so,' Mav said. 'I've got business to attend to. This time next week might be a different story.'

The old geek was lighting up a short stubby pipe. 'A couple of week's time you might not be in a position to leave. I hope you've made all the necessary arrangements with Doc Blandish and the undertaker?'

Mav grinned. 'I don't aim to take that journey in the immediate future and I'll leave Sheriff Bronco to make his own arrangements.'

The old man cackled.

* * *

Mav went in through the door of The Three Brothers and decided it was time to hit the hay. As he climbed the stairs he met the sewing-machine salesman who gave him a sideways glance and said in a whisper, 'Might I have word with you, Mr Mav?'

'Fire away,' Mav said.

The sewing-machine salesman gave a quick darting look all round. 'Not here,' he said quietly. 'You know walls have ears.'

'Why don't you step inside my room?' Mav said. 'We could have a private conversation in there.'

It was a small room but quite comfortable for a man who spent most of his time on the trail. There were two chairs and a bed. Mav sat down on one of the chairs and the sewing-machine salesman sat nervously on the other.

'What had you in mind?' Mav asked.

The sewing machine salesman was moving his interlaced fingers ceaselessly. 'I wanted to warn you, I believe you are in great danger,' he said.

'If you mean the sheriff wants to run me out of town, I think I know that already.'

The sewing-machine salesman gave him a twisted smile. 'That sheriff means to kill you. I heard them talking about it earlier this evening.'

'You mean like when we meet in the ring?'

The salesman leaned forward earnestly. 'If you want my opinion he means to kill you like he killed the others.'

'Which others?'

'All those men they couldn't account for lying up on Boot Hill, including Jed Arnold and Obediah Bead's brother Joe.'

Mav remembered what Obediah Bead had told him about the Stinking Ridge incident when Joe Bead had been killed by an unknown gunman.

'Are you telling me that Sheriff Bronco killed Joe Bead?' Mav asked.

'Not so loud!' the salesman protested. 'Yes,' he whispered earnestly. 'Bronco killed Joe and Obediah knows it. Joe was the only one in this family that really stuck out against Bronco and that's why Bronco killed him. No man who humiliates Bronco ever lives to tell the tale. After Bronco has given you a beating in the ring, even if he drives you out of town, you'll die somewhere out on the trail in mysterious circumstances.' He paused to take a couple of deep breaths. 'Now,' he continued, 'Obediah wants revenge and he doesn't have the courage to kill Bronco himself. So he's betting on you to do it for him. That's why he invited you to stay at The Three Brothers. Like I said, I heard Bronco and Bunce talking about it this evening.'

'Who's Bunce?'

'Bunce is a big rancher around here. He and Bronco aim to own the whole town. Bunce wants to run the MacKinleys off their land. That's one of the reasons there's so much bad blood in Pure Water.'

'And that's why Pure Water is call 'Perdition',' Mav speculated.

'Well, that's true as well,' the sewing-machine salesman agreed.

'Well, thanks for the warning,' Mav said. 'And why are you telling me this?'

The salesman tapped his fingers together with agitation. 'I'm telling you this because I don't like to see a brave man broken. To warn you, I guess, that you're caught in the middle and Bronco wants you dead, one way or the other.'

'Well, thanks again,' Mav said.

'I'm leaving town early tomorrow,' the salesman said. 'It's not too good for business here, anymore.'

To Mav that sounded like one big understatement.

5

Next morning the sewing machine salesman had gone. He left after an early breakfast to catch the stage. Mav gathered that his order book wasn't exactly overflowing with orders but, after his whispered message to Mav, he had probably decided that pulling out was his best option.

Mav went to the livery stable to pick up Huckleberry and Jed Arnold's flea-bitten nag.

'So you've decided to ride out,' the old geek said.

'Just taking a look at the country,' Mav replied laconically.

As he mounted up, he saw a string of fine-looking horses, maybe twenty or more, being herded down Main Street by Sam MacKinley and two of his hands. MacKinley greeted him with a wave and a tight smile. Then he reined in and let his hands ride on with the bunch of horses.

'So,' he said, 'I heard what happened. They say two men died outside Maisie's place. One was shot by the sheriff. Did you see that?'

'I saw Arnold die,' Mav said. 'Two bullets in his chest from close range. He wasn't even holding his gun.'

MacKinley's lip tightened. 'That's a bad business,' he said. 'What are you doing with that piece of crow bait hoss?' He was referring to Arnold's flea-bitten nag.

'That's Jed Arnold's horse,' Mav said. 'Nobody knows what to do with him, so I thought of saving him from being meat for the crows like you said.'

MacKinley gave him a quick sidelong glance. 'You got a fine piece of horse flesh there yourself,' he said referring to Huckleberry.

'You treat a horse right, he doesn't let you down,' Mav replied.

'You good with horses?' the rancher asked.

'Worked with them once in the Panhandle area,' Mav informed him. 'I got on with them well enough.'

'Got a delivery down at the Big Elk Ranch,' MacKinley said. 'They like good horses down there. You got nothing better to do, why don't you ride along with me? We could talk a little and maybe do some kind of a deal. One of my hands lit out yesterday. So I might offer you a job if you had a mind to it.'

'That might be a big gamble for you, Mr MacKinley. I've just been told I'm a marked man around here.'

'I'll take that chance,' MacKinley said.

They were riding past the sheriff's office and Bill Bronco came out on to the sidewalk to watch them through his narrowed eyes. Mav gave him an ironic salute but the sheriff made no response. Mav noticed that he was all tooled up with two six shooters.

'Looks in a mean mood,' MacKinley said.

'That's when I like him best,' Mav remarked with a grin.

*   *   *

'Thought you might be part of that play-acting bunch,' MacKinley said as they rode along together. 'They seem to think you're an OK guy, especially that woman Gladness. She has a high regard for you.'

'Stayed in the house with her in Cimarron once,' Mav admitted. 'We got along together fine.'

MacKinley greeted that comment with a slight lifting of the eyebrow. 'They're doing the show in one of my barns, you know. There's a honky-tonk piano out there. Mostly out of tune but Joe Basnett says he can fix it up. My wife, Jess, has a particular liking for theatricals. Good for the kids, she says. So I go along with it.'

'You think the townspeople will come along?'

'Oh, they'll come,' MacKinley affirmed.

'Nothing else to do. Pure Water used to be sort of holy, a kind of mission place, but things are changing since Peter Bead left. Of course, some people don't like that, particularly the Reverend Montague Means, that Bible-bashing gentleman.' MacKinley had an edge of bitterness to his grin.

They were soon riding through undulating country with a series of bluffs on their right and open prairie on their left.

'Purty country this,' MacKinley remarked. 'Best place in the world, I reckon.'

'How long have you been in the horse-rearing business?' Mav asked him.

'Since just before I decided to settle down and get married,' the rancher replied. 'I moved out here and the town kind of grew up around me.'

'I saw a sign out there said 'The way to Perdition',' Mav said.

'That's what some folks say since Bronco took over as sheriff. Should be Pure Water. Travellers stopped here about fifty years back. They found a spring. That's how it got its name. They figured it would be a good place to stay. Obediah Bead and some other people decided to put down their roots here.'

'Now you've got poison ivy in the shape of Bill Bronco,' Mav remarked ironically.

MacKinley raised his head and was about to speak when there was a sharp crack from way up on the right and one of the horses reared up and fell with its legs kicking in the air.

'What the hell?' said MacKinley, but, before he could say more, the whole bunch of horses had reared up and stampeded in a cloud of dust. There was a deal of shouting and MacKinley's two waddies took off after them. But Mav's horse Huckleberry was well trained. Though he had his ears pricked up he kept himself still and the flea-bitten nag followed his example.

MacKinley's horse was prancing round and MacKinley was straining his eyes towards the bluffs when there was another shot which took his hat clean off his head and sent it bowling away across the prairie until it came to rest on a juniper bush.

Mav had reached for his Winchester and yanked it out of its sheath. 'You'd better go get those horses under control,' he said before another shot came from above and the bullet whined close by his head.

'Those bastards mean to get us,' he said. 'They want more than the horses.' He was trying to pin-point the bush-whacker's position when he saw the form of a man rising from behind a rock. He raised his Winchester, steadied it, and fired a couple of shots. 'Not much chance,' he said. 'Out of range. Those sidewinders have got heavy artillery. You can tell by that bam bam noise.'

'What do you suggest?' MacKinley asked him.

'I know what I aim to do,' Mav said. 'I'm going right up there to get a fix on them. I figure they had second thoughts and have decided to high tail it. You'd better look after your horses, see they get safely through to that Big Elk ranch.'

Now the stampeding horses were quite a way off, trailing a cloud dust, and the two hands were riding wildly in pursuit.

'Those boys can manage,' MacKinley said with his jaw set. 'I'm coming with you. I want to know who we're up against here.'

There was nothing they could do for the horse lying dead. So they circled round the bluff, looking for where the bushwhackers had made their escape.

'Not much chance we could catch up on them?' Mav said.

'Not with that flea-bitten hoss in tow,' MacKinley said sceptically.

Mav slowed down, looking for signs. 'This is where they rode,' he said. 'Looks like there were three of them.'

'Three against two,' MacKinley said. 'That's good enough odds for me. They probably figure we won't trail them anyway.'

Mav was looking out between the

bluffs and he could see the dust rising where the bushwhackers were riding away. He pictured them laughing to themselves and that riled him up. 'I'm going to trail them anyway,' he said.

'That case, we'll ride together,' MacKinley said. 'Those boys can manage the horses on their own.'

'Then we ride together,' Mav agreed. 'But first I'm going up there to have a look see where they were shooting from.'

They rode up through the chaparral and poked around among the boulders. Mav was looking for a likely spot and, after a minute or two, he found it. He dismounted and began examining the area. Then he stooped and retrieved what he'd been searching for, a shell case from a rifle. 'That's what I thought,' he said, holding the shell case out to MacKinley.

MacKinley took it and examined it closely. 'That's a real big piece of artillery like you said,' he agreed.

'I figure it's from one of those Snider

rifles,' Mav speculated. 'Probably German or British, something from the army.'

MacKinley was down on his hunkers examining the shell case. 'How do you figure this?'

Mav was also squatting close to the rock. 'With a weapon like that those sidewinders could have sat up here and taken us out. Something tells me they were hired men. Either they wanted to scare us off or they thought they'd done enough.'

'Then who was their paymaster?' Sam MacKinley reflected.

'Could be your friend Bunce,' Mav suggested.

'We'll learn that when we find the man with the Snider,' Mav said.

* * *

They rode on between the bluffs, following the trail left by the bushwhackers who had made no attempt to hide their tracks.

'My guess is they won't expect us to

trail them,' Mav said. 'In an hour, maybe a little more, they'll think they got clean away. They'll stop and sit around for a while, eating and drinking and smoking their quirlies.'

'Tell you something,' MacKinley said after a while. 'I've been considering matters. Instinct tells me if I was those prairie rattlers I'd be taking my ease in a gulch I know just a mile ahead. It's nice and shady there and with good water for the horses, just the place for a taking a nap out of the sun.'

'If that hunch is right,' Mav said, 'we could maybe sneak up on them, give them a welcome party and taste of their own medicine.'

They rode on slowly for another half a mile. The sun was now well up in the sky and MacKinley was glad he had stopped to retrieve his hat which had quite a substantial hole right through it. An inch lower and it would have blasted a hole right through his temple.

'We'll stop here,' he said quietly. 'A good place for the horses to rest up in the shade of these junipers.'

They tethered their horses, gave them water from Mav's stained stetson, and left them to feed on whatever was available. Then they loped forward from bush to bush, pausing to listen from time to time. At first, Mav thought it might be a fool's errand, but, as they drew close to the gulch, he realized that MacKinley was a man of good instincts especially when he heard the snicker of a horse and caught a snatch of human laughter. Those bushwhackers were there all right, taking their ease in the shade.

Mav and MacKinley stopped for a brief consultation.

'What do we do?' Mav whispered.

'What we do is we creep up, look down from above, and frighten the shits out of them,' MacKinley said with a quiet chuckle.

The two men got down on their bellies and elbowed their way forward with their Winchesters in front of them. As they approached the ridge they took off their hats and elbowed forward to peer over the edge. As Mav had deduced there were three bushwhackers. Two were half sprawled beside an Indian blanket playing five card stud. The other, a lean and hungry type, sat under a stunted bush cleaning the Snider rifle that had inflicted the damage. He wore a Smith & Wesson in a holster on his hip.

Mav and MacKinley exchanged glances and nodded. Mav was ready to make his move but he stopped when the bush-whackers started talking again.

'Thought you claimed to be a dead shot with that cannon of yourn,' one of the card players said.

The man who was lovingly cleaning his Snider looked up quickly. 'I can shoot in the right circumstances,' he said in a nut-brown voice.

'What, like when you're at the fairground?' the other card player jeered.

'I could have taken out both those waddies if I had a mind to it,' the Snider man boasted.

'Then why didn't you?' the fatter of the two cowboys retorted. 'I thought that's what you were hired to do.'

'Easy as shelling peas,' the Snider man drawled. 'I was hired to scare the shits out of them, specially the guy who calls himself Mav.'

'You shot up the wrong man,' the fat one laughed. 'That's unless you mean the horse.'

The two cowboys were rolling about laughing.

Mav motioned to MacKinley and they drew back from the edge of the gulch. 'You know these *hombres*?' he whispered.

'I know them,' MacKinley said in reply. 'Two of them worked for me as wranglers one time. Murphy and Stamford. I don't know the guy with the big artillery piece. He's probably a hired gunman.'

'What do you reckon to do?' Mav asked him.

'I have half a mind to blast them to kingdom come,' MacKinley whispered hoarsely. 'Pepper them full of holes.

That's what they wanted to do to us.'

'That way we don't find out who hired them,' Mav said.

MacKinley thought about that for a moment and then nodded. 'OK, then we make our move and take them in.'

They elbowed their way up to the ridge again.

The two men in the poker game were still laughing and pushing one another around.

'Tell you something,' Stamford crowed. 'Did you see how MacKinley's hat flew off his head just like a bird.'

The man with the rifle chuckled. 'A little lower I could have spattered his brains with a single shot.'

'That would have been something to see,' the fat man roared as he rolled about laughing.

'Then, why didn't you? Stamford asked.

'You go for the wranglers,' Mav whispered. 'I'll take care of the big boy.' He pushed his Winchester forward and fired a round above the gunman's head. That gulch acted like a funnel and the

101

noise of the shot seemed to ricochet from one side to the other and then back again.

The two cowboys spun round and made a grab for their side arms while the man with the Snider darted away as quickly as a snake in a fire and drew his Smith & Wesson. That man was fast and, before Mav could fire a second shot, he felt hot lead flying close to his head. The Snider man was up on his feet in a second, palm fanning his gun and short stabs of yellow flame came spurting from the barrel.

Another shot whined close to Mav's head.

Sam MacKinley was pumping hot lead at the other two as they skittered away into the scrub for cover.

That Snider man is making a damned fool of me, Mav thought as he fired another round. The Snider man spun round and sat down abruptly.

The two cowboys dropped their guns and held up their arms. 'OK,' shouted Murphy. 'OK. So you got the drop on us.'

'It's what you do that matters,' Mav told them. 'You just stand nice and easy, unbuckle your gun-belts and let them drop.'

They moved like men in a slow-motion pantomime and did as they were told. Murphy squinted up at MacKinley. 'Why all that gun play, Mr MacKinley?' he asked.

'Maybe it's because I don't like the company you keep,' MacKinley said grimly.

Stamford said nothing: he was too busy trembling with fear.

The gunman said nothing. He was too busy pressing his hand against his wounded arm.

'And who might you be?' Mav asked him.

'I'm just just a man riding through,' the gunman said.

'You carry a mighty useful piece of weaponry for a man riding through,' Mav remarked.

'Useful for shooting rats,' the man jeered.

'Well, Mr Rat Catcher, do you have a

name?' Mav asked him. This man's playing for time, he thought. A man who plays for time has a bad purpose in view.

'I know who you are,' the man said. 'You're Mav short for Maverick, alias Jesse Bolder. I believe you're wanted back east for murder. And you killed Big Bravo and Coyote Ben and the rest of them in Cimarron. That's who you are.'

MacKinley gave Mav a quick glance as though he didn't believe what he was hearing.

'OK,' Mav said to the man. 'So you don't have a name. You just like to shoot at men and horses from a high bluff. That takes a heap of courage.'

Stamford, who was shaking, suddenly spoke in a high quavering voice. 'Mr MacKinley, we didn't mean no harm back there. I never fired a shot. I never meant nobody nothing bad. You hear me?'

'I hear you good, Stamford,' MacKinley said. 'In which case you must be a reformed character.'

Murphy started to laugh and Stamford joined in with a hysterical giggle and that was when the man with the Snider made his second move. Despite his wound he spun round suddenly with something in his hand. There was a flash and a crack as he fired the Derringer at Mav. He was quick but speed and the pain of this wound made him inaccurate. Without stopping to think Mav fired his Winchester and the gunman reared right into the bush. He shuddered violently and lay still.

'My gawd, you killed him!' Murphy gasped.

Stamford said nothing; he was too busy looking for a way of escape. Murphy was looking about in dismay but he stayed where he was with his hands in the air.

Mav and MacKinley tucked their Winchesters under their arms and made their way down into the gulch.

As MacKinley approached, Stamford held up his hands. 'Don't shoot, Mr MacKinley,' he pleaded. 'I didn't mean no harm. I thought they just wanted to put the frighteners on you.'

'They sure put them on you.' MacKinley prodded him with his Winchester.

Mav went over to the nameless man with the Snider and looked down into his eyes. The man seemed to stare at him with reproach but he was quite dead.

'You killed him!' Murphy gasped.

* * *

'You mind telling me who this is?' Mav said with his gun on Murphy.

Murphy shook his head. 'I never knew his name,' he said.

'But you do know who hired him,' Mav asserted.

Murphy shook his head. 'I can't tell you that.'

'I think you'd better tell me that.' Mav raised the Winchester and pointed it at Murphy's head.

'I can tell you,' squeaked Stamford.

'Sure you can,' MacKinley said. 'Why don't we just set ourselves down and talk nice and easy?' He motioned with his Winchester. 'And keep your hands where we can see them in case you get any strange ideas.'

The two would-be killers sat down on the blanket with their hands in front of them. MacKinley sat on a smooth rock, facing them with his Winchester across his knees. Mav rested against another rock where he could see the two wranglers.

'Now it's confession time, boys,' MacKinley said. 'Time to spill the beans.'

The two wranglers exchanged uneasy glances.

'And if you're going to tell me you didn't mean any harm, save that for the judge.' He made a slight motion with his Winchester.

Neither of the two wranglers seemed anxious to speak. No doubt Stamford was uneasy in his pants. After a moment Murphy decided to put in a word.

'Well now, Mr MacKinley, Luke and

me was just acting as guides. We didn't rightly know what was going to happen.'

'Is that why you were joking about Mr MacKinley's hat flying off like a bird?' Mav asked.

'That was just horsing around,' Murphy said.

'OK, then,' MacKinley nodded. 'Now tell me who hired you, what they paid, and why.'

'Just as long as you accept that me and Luke never fired a shot. It was Jude Janvers who did the shooting.'

'Jude Janvers,' Mav said. 'Who hired Janvers?'

'Well, I guess you know who hired Janvers,' Murphy said.

'Why don't you tell me?' Mav said.

The two wranglers exchanged uneasy glances again, but this time Stamford responded. 'Why Sheriff Bronco hired Janvers,' he said.

Now Mav and MacKinley exchanged glances and neither of them seemed surprised.

'You know Bronco is a most revengeful man,' Murphy said. 'When Mr Mav lashed out at him like that he was boiling over for revenge. I know you challenged him to a fist fight in the ring but he wants you dead.'

'But back here Janvers fired his second shot at me,' Sam MacKinley said.

Murphy didn't know the answer to that or he didn't want to give it.

Though Stamford was still shaking slightly, he proved to be a little more forthcoming. 'It's about more than Bronco,' he said. 'It's about the Bunce outfit.'

'So, come clean,' MacKinley said. 'You're working for Bronco and Bunce, both of them.'

'Tell me about Bunce?' Mav said.

MacKinley shook his head. 'Bunce runs a big spread about two miles out of town. He's claiming water rights down in Blue Gully. Wants to drive me out of business. This has been going on for some time. Bunce wants me off the range.'

Mav nodded. 'That's what I heard. So Bronco and Bunce are in league together. Is that the way it is?'

'Bunce and Bronco are buddies from way back,' Sam MacKinley said. 'They want to own the whole town and the range as well. So that explains why Jude Janvers was hired to kill me or put the frighteners on me and you.'

'Looks like we're in this together, up to our necks,' Mav speculated.

6

An hour later a small cavalcade rode into Perdition. In the lead was Sam MacKinley trailing a horse with a man lying dead face down across the saddle. They were followed by two men with their hands tied across their saddle-horns. After that came Mav riding on his horse Huckleberry, trailing Jed Arnold's flea-bitten nag.

The whole cavalcade drew up outside the sheriff's office and Mav took down the body of Jude Janvers and laid it none too gently on the sidewalk. A number of citizens crowded round, including some children who gawped at the body in some astonishment.

'Is that man really dead?' one of the girls asked fearfully.

'Well, he sure ain't sleeping,' a pimply boy replied. 'Can't you see the blood and the bullet hole in his chest?'

Sheriff Bronco was sitting in his office talking to a man Mav hadn't seen before. When he heard the commotion, Bronco got up and peered out of the door. He saw two woebegone cowboys and a body lying face-up on the sidewalk amidst a swarm of flies. Beyond them on Main Street stood Sam MacKinley and Mav, both with shooters trailing at their sides.

'What's this?' Bronco enquired, looking down at the corpse.

'Thought you might know him,' Mav said. 'They tell me he's a friend of yours. Name of Janvers, so they tell me.'

'Blew a hole in my Stetson way back there,' MacKinley informed Bronco. 'He killed one of my best horses, too. It was just about the last deed he did, otherwise he'd still be in the land of the living.'

The man Bronco had been talking to in the office suddenly emerged.

'Why, Mr Bunce!' exclaimed MacKinley wryly. 'So here you are talking to the sheriff. Thought we'd bring you back

your boys, deliver them safely to you.'
He gave Murphy a shove in the back
and the fat man lurched forward suddenly.

Stamford had his mouth wide open
and he was shaking again.

Bunce was a big man, almost as tall
as Bronco, but his muscles had run
away to seed. He had a large walrus-
type moustache and bushy side-whiskers
and a gold chain stretched across his
vest. He obviously considered himself a
person of some social standing.

'What's the meaning of this?' he
demanded, looking down at what was
left of Janvers.

'Self-defence,' MacKinley said. 'Tried
to kill us and we had no alternative.'

'That's nothing on my account,'
Bunce blustered.

'That's your story,' Sam MacKinley
replied. 'But these two mutton heads
say different. They say you paid Janvers
to pick us off and these two down-at-
heel *hombres* were hired as guides since
they know the country.'

Bunce gave the two hired men a scornful glare. 'That's just a load of horse shit,' he proclaimed. 'Why should I hire men to guide this man to put the frighteners on you. It doesn't make sense anyway you look at it. I never saw this man Janvers in my life before and how would I know which way you would be riding with those horses anyway?'

'I would say you were remarkably well-informed, Mr Bunce,' MacKinley said. 'I didn't mention frighteners, I said attempted murder. And plenty of people would know we were riding to the Big Elk spread.'

'So what?' Bunce said, sticking his paunch out aggressively.

'So this,' MacKinley replied. 'You send your sidekicks to shoot at us from cover, your sidekicks are going to get what's coming to them . . . and that goes for you as well.'

'That sounds mighty like a threat to me.' Bunce braced himself with his hand close to the Colt he carried in a holster on his right hip.

Bronco was standing in his usual boastful way with his thumbs hooked into his belt and his chest puffed out. He was looking not at MacKinley but at Mav. 'Ever since you rode into this town there's been nothing but trouble, Bolder,' he said.

'That's true, Sheriff,' Mav rejoined. 'And I think you know who's responsible for that trouble.' Mav's hand rested on his holster. The people who had crowded out of their shops and saloons expecting to see another showdown drew back in case a stray bullet went their way, but the tension was eased suddenly when someone asked: 'What's been happening here?' and the bearded figure of the Reverend Montague Means stepped forward and peered down at Janver's stiffened body. 'Why doesn't someone have the decency to cover this corpse's face. It's just indecent to let it lie here attracting the flies while you argue the whys and wherefores.'

Luckily the undertaker's assistant

was standing by and he hurried forward to cover the corpse's face with a gunny sack.

'That's better,' the Reverend Means responded. 'You know, men, what the good book says?' He raised his right hand as if about to bestow a blessing. He was wearing a long black frock coat which, together with his flowing white beard, made him look like the the Angel of Death himself.

Now the funeral director showed up and Murphy and Samford took the opportunity to melt into the crowd.

'You haven't seen the end of this,' Bunce said as Sam MacKinley and Mav mounted up again.

'I'm sure you're right on that, Mr Bunce. This is just the beginning,' MacKinley acknowledged.

Mav looked over his shoulder and he saw Bill Bronco glaring at him like a fiend from hell.

★ ★ ★

'Tell you what,' Sam MacKinley said tight-lipped as they rode away. 'I think we might have a range war on our hands here. Those mean bastards won't stop until they drive us out of the territory and that means both you and me.'

Mav glanced at him thoughtfully. 'You could be right there. I think somebody put a curse on me. Like every town I ride into, people start getting shot. It must be the devil himself or some evil spirit.'

'Maybe not,' MacKinley speculated. 'Maybe the devil's here already and you just poked him with a stick. You ever thought of it like that?'

Mav gave a wry grin. 'That doesn't make me some kind of saint, does it?'

'Never met a saint in my life before,' MacKinley said. 'Think I'd be a mite uncomfortable if I did.' He leaned back in the saddle. 'I have a suggestion to make, Mav, a proposal, I guess you could call it.'

'If it's marriage you mean, forget it,'

Mav rejoined. 'I'm way too young. When I'm eighty I might consider it if you can cook and make the beds.'

MacKinley twisted his mouth in a grin. 'Tell you what, I don't think you should go back to The Three Brothers.'

'Why not? Obediah Bead's wife's cooking is good.'

'Cooking's one thing. Shooting or knifing in the night is another thing altogether.'

Mav nodded thoughtfully. 'That could be messy,' he agreed, 'But the Reverend Montague Means is there to read me psalms and wave his hands over me.'

'Yes, just like he did to Janvers,' MacKinley said. 'Listen good. I'm short of hands at the ranch right now. You're good with horses — I've seen that and I like it. And you're a man with his head screwed on to his shoulders right. Why don't I offer you a job? You could move into the bunkhouse and be my top hand right away. I need a good man by my side. Not much pay but prospects for the right man. Cooking's good, too, maybe even tastier than at The Three Brothers.' He gave a broad wink. 'Not me, my wife. Another thing, you'd be closer to those actor friends, at least when you're not on the trail. I've got a hunch those actors are going to need someone to protect them when the fire of hell comes raining down on them.'

That made Mav sit up a little. He hadn't thought of the trouble that might be coming to his actor friends. 'I think you got yourself a deal,' he said.

The two men turned in the saddle and shook hands.

★　★　★

When Mav checked out of the The Three Brothers, Obediah Bead gave him a look of mild surprise. 'So you don't find us to your taste?' he asked in a slight tone of irony.

'I like it well enough,' Mav said. 'Your wife's cooking is right out of a book. She should become an author and write up her recipes, 'The Three Brothers Cook Book'. Like I told you, I've been looking for a job and I think I found one.'

'Nothing to do with Bronco and Bunce, I guess?' Obediah Bead said ironically.

'Funny you said that,' Mav replied. 'If I stayed right here I think I might be tempted to put those two ornery bastards under the sod and you wouldn't want that, would you? Could spoil your reputation for good food.'

Obediah Bead gave him a strange look, something between surprise and approval. 'Ever thought of becoming a sheriff?' he said.

Mav shook his head. 'I've had one or two offers but so far I've resisted them. I like working with horses better than human trash. I think I might have a gift for it.'

'I think you're way too modest,' Bead said. 'Could be you have more gifts than you think.' Mav noticed that he had a strange twinkle in his eye.

* * *

When Mav stepped into the barn at the MacKinley place the first thing he heard was Gladness singing at the piano. Joe Basnett was accompanying her, not brilliantly but competently. At least he hit the right notes and played the most appropriate chords reasonably quietly so as not to drown out the singer's sweet voice.

Mav stood in the doorway and listened and, to him, it was like the song of a nightingale. He didn't know what the song was, something like 'love's old sweet song', but somehow he responded to it. He had never thought of himself as a particularly sentimental man (life was much too hard for that) but when he heard that beautiful voice something made the roots of his hair tingle.

When Gladness saw him framed in the doorway she stopped singing in mid flow as though something had hit her right between the eyes. Joe Basnett played a few more chords and then stopped with his hands straddling the keyboard and looked round at Mav.

'So it's you,' Gladness murmured quietly.

'I believe it is,' Mav replied. Indeed, he had never seen Gladness in this light before, or heard her voice singing so sweetly.

'You have a beautiful voice,' he said. 'Where did you learn that?'

'Gladness didn't need to learn it,' Joe Basnett said. 'She has natural talent.'

Gladness moved away from the piano and came towards Mav like a woman in a dream. My God! he thought, have you ever seen such a change in a woman! He remembered the Gladness he had seen in that house that was falling apart in Cimarron. She had been dressed in working overalls as she mended the gutters and painted the boards. But this was a different woman altogether.

Now she was only a few feet away, looking up at him. 'I hear they've been shooting at you,' she said.

'That's all over now,' Mav said.

'And you killed a man,' she said.

'Not much choice,' he replied. 'He tried to shoot us. We had to shoot back.'

Mav spared her the details. 'Sam MacKinley has offered me a job with his horses. I'm moving in right now.'

Joe Basnett had risen from the piano and he stood, wide-eyed and perplexed, looking towards them. He was probably thinking about the time his partner was killed by the Bravo and Coyote Ben bunch back in Cimarron and he had to be rescued by the Comanche. 'If there's going to be shooting, maybe we should forget this whole business of putting on our show and move on to another town.' His voice was high-pitched and wobbly.

Gladness turned to him quickly and said: 'No, Joe. We can't give way to those bullies. We have to go on.'

'I think you're right,' Mav said. 'You give way to bullies, more bullies come along and the world gets to be a nightmare.'

'I agree to that,' Sadie said. She and

Queenie Caryl had just come into the barn.

★ ★ ★

Someone was knocking hell out of a triangle and the shout echoed among the outbuildings. 'Supper's up, come and get it!' They all trooped up to the big ranch house where Sam MacKinley's wife Sarah was waiting to serve up the chow. In the big room they sat at a long pine table, the four actors, the five ranch hands, Mav, and Sam and Sarah MacKinley and the two kids.

To Mav's surprise, before they all pounced on their food, Sarah MacKinley announced that her husband would be saying a word of grace. Sam MacKinley, looking slightly embarrassed, delivered a quick mumbled prayer, ending with amen to which they all gave a murmuring response.

'This is a right religious town,' Mav said, sitting down next to Sam MacKinley. The two children, a boy and a girl, were chattering together and discussing the day's events. From time to time they gave Mav a keen and inquisitive look.

'They know all about it,' Sam said. 'You're the hero of the hour.'

'Nice of you to say so,' Mav rejoined and Gladness gave him an anxious glance from the other side of the table.

'I hear that big bag of blubber Murphy and that quivering mess of a man Stamford gunned down on you,' one of the hands, a tall rangy character, said from the other end of the table.

MacKinley nodded briefly. The two waddies who had herded the horses to the Big Elk Ranch were back safe and they wanted to hear all about it. Sam MacKinley told them about the killing of Janvers and they laughed.

'Heard of Janvers,' one of them said. 'Bushwhacking is just his style but he poked his gun out once too often this time.'

That caused a general laugh around the table, but Mav noticed that Sarah and Gladness didn't join in.

'There's going to be a heap of

trouble,' Sarah said. 'Bunce and Bronco won't be happy till they ride us right out of the county and rub our faces in the dust.'

'That's not going to happen,' Sam MacKinley assured her.

At that moment another hand who had been tending the horses popped his head in at the door. 'Excuse me, Mr MacKinley,' he said. 'There's a whole bunch of men down by the gate with the sheriff, said they want to talk to you and will you come down to the boundary line right away?'

* * *

Sam MacKinley wiped his mouth on a napkin Sarah insisted on providing. Then he stood up from the table. 'It's starting already,' he said quietly to Mav. Mav was already on his feet.

'I'd like to come with you,' he said.

'Me too,' said the tall rangy hand who had asked about Janvers.

The other hands were already on their

126

feet, eager to join in and see the fun.

But Sam MacKinley flapped his hand discouragingly. 'No call for that, boys. This is for Mav and me. Too many would spook the horses. I think we should play this slow and steady.'

The boys sat down again reluctantly.

Nevertheless, MacKinley and Mav strapped on their shooters. Gladness was studying Mav with a look of profound concern. Sarah MacKinley hushed everybody up and told them not to make a mountain out of a mole hill.

As MacKinley and Mav started down the dusty track towards the arch with the buffalo horns, they saw a whole bunch of men on horseback, among them Bill Bronco and the rancher Bunce.

'Looks like they've been talking things over,' MacKinley muttered. 'Decided to bring out the big guns.'

'What guns would they be?' Mav asked sardonically. Most of the accompanying force were obviously cow-punchers but one or two could have been hired gunmen.

'Janvers wasn't the only one,' Sam MacKinley said. 'I've seen most of these waddies before, Bunce's hired hands, but those two at the back of the bunch look pretty mean to me.'

Mav had already decided that for himself. The two mean-looking *hombres* that Sam had referred to wore dark leather vests and dark brown Stetsons. Though they weren't close enough to smell, Mav guessed they had the wreak of death about them. They could have been the twins from Hell.

Sam and Mav walked right up to the entrance and stood surveying the ugly throng.

'So, you want something, Mr Bronco?' Sam said.

Sitting on his horse, Bronco looked like a giant in a fairy tale and he glared down at Sam with a twisted cynical grin. 'Something I forgot to mention,' he said.

'And what would that be?' Sam asked him.

Bronco's horse edged to one side.

'Like I've seen posters up around town advertising a show you're hoping to put on in that there barn of yours.'

'Well, you've seen right,' Sam replied.

Bronco gigged his horse around a bit more as if to emphasize his point. 'Happen you might know,' he said, 'you can't run any kind of show in this town without paying a fee.'

'What fee is that?' Sam asked.

'Depends on the show,' the sheriff retorted. 'Could be as much as five hundred dollars or more.'

'On whose authority?' Sam asked.

'That's for me to decide,' Bronco said. 'You want to go ahead with that show, you pay me five hundred dollars flat. Then I issue a written authorisation for the show provided it's good and clean and good for the family. From what I heard your so-called show might not pass the test.'

The cowpunchers behind him started to snigger in anticipation. The two sinister-looking *hombres* in dark hats remained poker faced.

'Tell you something,' Sam MacKinley said. 'This is my ranch. It might be close to the edge of town but it's my property. If I want to hold a little party in my barn for the entertainment of my friends and neighbours, that's what I'm gonna do, and nothing you say will stop me.' He raised his voice slightly. 'You hear that good, Mr Bronco?'

Bronco nodded as though he was pleased with the response. 'Well, we'll see about that, Mr MacKinley. We'll see about that.' He turned to Bunce and his cowpunchers. 'I hope you all heard what the man said. I might need witnesses to that later on.'

Bunce spoke up loud and clear, 'We heard what he said,' he croaked.

'Sure did,' some of the cowpunchers murmured and nodded in agreement.

'Just remember that,' Bronco said. Then he held up his hand and the whole band wheeled round and rode away in a swirl of dust.

Except for the two men in dark hats. They edged forward and came close to

MacKinley and Mav. Mav saw that they were both hard men, well tooled up as though they meant business. One of them, a lean streak of a man, looked down at Mav. 'I guess you must be Jesse Bolder who calls himself Mav,' he said in a deep matter-of-fact tone.

'Who wants to know?' Mav asked.

'The devil wants to know,' the man said in a gritty voice. 'Make sure I get my sights on the right man.'

'You got the right man,' Mav said. 'Now perhaps you'll be good enough to tell me who you might be in case I mistake you for some kind of desert rat?'

The two men with the dark hats exchanged glances.

'You want to know I'm Jake Fuller,' the lean one said.

Mav shook his head. 'Don't think I've heard of a Jake Fuller.'

'You will,' the man said. 'My brother was Ben Fuller. Some people called him Coyote Ben, the man you killed near Cimarron. Maybe you remember him.'

Mav gave a formal nod. 'Sure, I remember him.' He could have added that Ben Fuller was one of the meanest *hombres* he had ever met but he let that go for the moment.

'Tell you one thing,' Jake Fuller added. 'When you take your final breath, Ben Fuller is the last thing you'll remember. Just remember that, Bolder.'

'I'll bear that in mind,' Mav said.

The two men turned their horses and rode away down the trail back towards Pure Water.

7

'Now you know just what you're getting yourself into,' Mav said as they walked back towards the ranch house.

'It seems that, one way or the other, you're not the most popular guy in the territory,' Sam said with a wry grin.

'That could be so,' Mav conceded. 'Seems like I have some kind of jinx on me like the devil was hanging on my shoulder.'

'Well, it ain't the worst devil in the world,' Sam said. 'And you know something. Bill Bronco and Bunce are dead afraid of anyone that stands up to them and they're fools as well.'

'Why do you say that?' Mav asked him. 'You some kind of brain doctor or something?'

Sam chuckled. 'Put it down to experience,' he said. 'I've met people like Bronco and Bunce before. There's no fool like a frightened fool. They try to bully their way through life but when the chips are down they're as scared as hell. That's why they hire others to spread their shit around. Like that Janvers. He might be pushing up the daisies but Bunce is cunning. So he hires two gunmen. Bunce knows what happened down Cimarron way. So he hires a grudge man like Jake Fuller and Smith Riley too.'

'Who's Smith Riley?'

'Smith Riley is the one who kept his mouth shut just now. But don't be fooled by that. Smith Riley is no sidekick. He has the venom of a whole box full of rattlers and he enjoys using it.'

'You mean you've met this Smith Riley before?'

Sam shook his head. 'I've seen him but I never met him personally. Some of my boys have encountered him in the past. You come across a critter like Riley you don't forget him in a hurry.'

This didn't exactly worry Mav

because he wasn't the worrying sort, but it did concentrate his mind somewhat. He thought of those actors again, especially Gladness. She had had a heap of trouble in the past, particularly when those Apache Indians had raided her farm and killed her husband and her two little children. That had left a deep scar on Gladness from which she would probably never recover fully.

He was still thinking about that as they drew close to the ranch house again. Gladness and Sarah MacKinley were standing close together with the two children watching their approach. They had followed the proceedings from the ramada and now they wanted a full report.

Sarah was a tall lean pioneering woman and she was not easily cowed. The boy and the girl were looking at their father with eager apprehensive eyes and Mav could see from the look in Gladness's eyes and from the way she had her hands on the girl's shoulder that she wanted to protect those kids like they were her own.

Sam MacKinley gave a full account of the confrontation to his wife without mentioning the two gunmen and what Jake Fuller had said to Mav.

'We give way to those bullies we might as well be dead,' Sarah said. She wasn't the woman to mince her words.

'That's why we're not going to give way,' Sam said, thrusting out his jaw. 'Come Saturday the show goes on like we planned. If those sidewinders try to make trouble they'll stir up a riot in the town.'

'So you think people will come to the show?' Gladness asked him.

'Oh, they'll come,' Sam said confidently. 'Nothing's going to stop them from coming.'

The sound of the actors rehearsing their lines came from the barn. 'Time I went,' Gladness said. 'I have to rehearse again.'

Dedication, Mav thought, those actors sure have dedication. He didn't know much about acting, though he had attended one or two shows back east with his mother when he was small. He was impressed by Gladness's dedication. Mav thought she sounded quite enthusiastic.

★ ★ ★

Mav was settled in the bunkhouse which, though primitive, was reasonably comfortable since Sarah MacKinley liked everything to be even and fair and in apple pie order.

Four of the hands were playing poker but the tall lean waddy who had joked about Janvers was lounging on his cot and smoking a hand-rolled quirly.

'So you're the new top hand?' he said, looking Mav up and down.

'Worked with horses most of my life,' Mav said. 'I like them better than most of the people I know.'

'I notice you have a particular liking for that horse Huckleberry of yours,' the man said. He stretched out a large spidery hand. 'Name's O'Leary,' he said. 'Daniel O'Leary.'

Mav gripped the offered hand and gave it a brief shake. 'Good to meet you, Daniel.'

The poker players laughed as though Mav had made some kind of joke.

'We heard you were good with a gun too,' one of them asked.

Mav didn't answered that directly. 'I carry a gun, but I don't care to use it unless I have to.'

'From what I heard you're quite useful when you have to be,' one of the others said.

'No use carrying a gun unless you're willing to use it,' Mav rejoined.

'Well, in my opinion you're going to have to use it a lot round here,' the first man said.

'As long as it's self-defence,' Mav said and that caused another round of laughter.

Daniel O'Leary, the lean man lying on the cot stirred himself again. 'Come sunrise, we're going up to Blue Gully,' he announced. 'Not far from here. A good place for good clean water. Sam likes to go there on a regular basis since Bunce has staked a claim to the place and wants to keep us out.'

'So you might have reason to use that gun of yours in self-defence,' one of the poker players joked.

Though there was no obvious objection to Mav's being the top wrangler the other hands did show a degree of envy since Mav had drifted in so unexpectedly.

* * *

Early next morning, Mav found himself riding beside Sam MacKinley with Daniel O'Leary and two of the card players, up towards Blue Gully. Blue Gully was some miles away towards the hills. It had been named Blue Gully some half a century earlier when an old-timer had stopped to scoop up water and, when he peered down into the creek, he not only saw his rippling bearded face but noticed that everything looked blue and shiny and friendly. So he decided to name it Blue Creek in Blue Gully. And that's what it had been ever since.

'Don't like to ask,' Sam said to Mav as they rode along with a bunch of horses, 'but do you aim to be blown about like tumbleweed for ever, or do you aim to settle down?'

Mav gave him a quizzical look. 'I'm not sure that settling down is my thing,' he said. 'Setting around in a rocking-chair smoking a pipe isn't exactly my style.'

'So you aim to ride the range till you get too old and stiff to fit into that rocking-chair you mention, do you?'

'I guess that'll be when I'm about stiff enough to fit into my pine box,' Mav said.

He rode on in silence for a while.

'You have something particular in mind?' he asked.

'Maybe something you won't want to hear,' Sam said. 'Too much like sticking your nose into another man's business and I'm not good at that.'

'Well, I give you full permission as a friend to stick your nose in wherever you have a mind to,' Mav said. 'Just as long as it isn't about money because right now the larder's bare.'

'I don't notice much,' Sam said. 'But my woman Sarah sees everything. I sometimes think she stares down a deep private well and sees things most folks don't have a hope of catching a glimpse of.'

'You mean she sees me down there swimming around?' Mav laughed.

'Sure, she sees you,' Sam said. 'And she sees other things too and other people. She tells me you've got company down there and you're not alone.'

'What kind of company?' Mav asked.

'Matter of fact, woman company.' Sam gave him a brief cock-eyed stare.

'Maybe that's the kind I like,' Mav said. 'Does Sarah see any particular woman swimming with me?'

'Of course I don't see anything myself,' Sam apologised. 'I'm not long sighted enough.'

'A man doesn't need to apologise for squinting a little,' Mav said. 'Who's the particular woman in question?'

'The woman Sarah sees swimming with you is Gladness,' Sam admitted.

He was just about to add that he thought Gladness was a very fine specimen of womankind when Daniel O'Leary drew up beside him and said, 'Sorry to butt in on your conversation, boss, but did you notice we're being tailed?'

'How many?' Sam asked.

'Difficult to say,' O'Leary said. 'Could be a whole bunch. I happened to catch the sun reflected off a telescope back there.'

Sam tightened his jaw. 'That'll be Bunce's chuckle-headed side-kicks,' he said.

'What do you want me to do, Boss?' O'Leary asked.

Sam turned to Mav. 'You think we should ride up and flush them out?' he said.

Mav shrugged. 'You want it, we'll do it.'

'My opinion, we should ride on to the creek,' Sam said.

O'Leary looked up and scanned the hills. 'Whatever you say. Just as long as you realize we're like roosting ducks down here. Those mean *hombres* could pick us off without any trouble at all.'

Sam shook his head. 'That's true enough. We just have to hope those varmints aren't quite set to start a shooting war yet.'

★ ★ ★

They rode on until they came within sight of Blue Creek. And then Sam raised his arm and they stopped. The horses were restive since they had caught the smell of sweet water in their nostrils but the boys circled round and stopped the whole bunch from going any further forward.

'So that's the way they want to play it,' Sam said, shading his eyes from the sun.

Strung out along the side to the creek was a string of barbed-wire attached to posts in the centre of which was a board with a notice on it painted in red.

Sam whistled between his teeth and drew the cavalcade to a halt. Then he rode forward to read the notice which said: 'THIS IS A PRIVATE CREEK. KEEP OFF AT YOUR PERAL.'

'At your peral,' O'Leary laughed. 'What's peral?'

'Peral is a kind of two-headed skunk that stinks from both ends,' Sam said.

'Well, at least they got that right,' O'Leary laughed.

Mav drew the Winchester from his saddle-holster and scanned the hills, steadying the weapon against his thigh.

'Despite the words, I figure this is getting serious,' O'Leary said. 'You know what it means, don't you, Boss?'

'I think it means war,' Mav agreed.

Sam was riding up and down inspecting the posts and the barbed wire. Then he rode back towards Mav.

'Bunce is getting himself in real deep

here,' he muttered between his teeth.

'Deep enough to drown himself in the creek,' Mav agreed. 'What do you aim to do?' Mav knew the answer before he asked the question.

Sam narrowed his eyes and looked around. Then he barked out his orders and two of the hands busied themselves demolishing the notice and ripping down the barbed wire. Then the horses were driven forward to drink their fill.

'This has been coming for a long time,' Sam muttered between gritted teeth, 'and now it's here.'

'Just like the devil on my shoulder,' Mav remarked. 'I warned you about that jinx.'

'That jinx could be mighty useful here,' Sam said.

Then they heard the sound of horses moving and, looking up, saw riders outlined on the other side of the creek, three, maybe four of them, among them Bunce himself and the two hired gunmen, Jake Fuller and Smith Riley who had been at the entrance of the MacKinley ranch the day before. The two gunmen were lined up with Bunce, one on each side just like they were propping him up. They had Winchester carbines lying across their saddles.

'What do you want here, MacKinley?' Bunce roared out. 'Can't you read a sign when you see it?'

'I read what's in good clear language and what's good and legal,' Sam said.

'This is good and legal,' Bunce retorted. 'I got it all written up and witnessed. This creek belongs to me all legal and sealed.'

'Well, I hope your legal advisors can spell out their words better than you, Bunce.'

Bunce shook his head. He obviously had no idea what Sam was referring to.

'What's peral? Is that some kind of rabid dog?' O'Leary asked.

'Peral is when a man gets shot taking an illegal drink in a creek,' Bunce shouted across the water.

'That's not peral,' Sam replied. 'That's just hogwash and you know it. My horses have been watering in this creek for the past twenty years gone by and you know that.'

'Not any more,' Bunce boasted. 'The past is catching up with you and this is the last time your horses drink here. And now you get those critters right out of my creek and take them back to your ranch pronto. You hear what I say?'

'I hear bullshit,' Sam replied.

The two hired gunmen raised their Winchesters and held them over their horse's heads. Mav had seen that move before and he knew that those two ornery *hombres* wouldn't think twice before shooting a man down if the money was right.

Mav cocked his gun and got ready for the inevitable showdown. He glanced at O'Leary and saw that he was all set to draw his gun too. 'You take Riley and I'll take Fuller,' he said out of the corner of his mouth.

'If there's gonna be shooting, I shoot first,' Sam said with his hand on the butt of his six shooter. 'And that means Bunce.'

Staring straight into Sam's eyes Bunce

seemed to sense his determination and Mav could see him falter. Bunce wasn't a fighting man himself and he liked others to do his dirty work for him, and dying wasn't part of his plan.

'I'm warning you, MacKinley,' Bunce said in a slightly less confident tone. 'If you don't get off this creek I have some friends who can make you. So you pull out right now before things get serious.'

Mav was watching the two gunmen and he stared straight into the relentless eyes of Fuller. There would be no giving way there, he figured. If you're forced to shoot a man, do it quick and clean before he shoots at you. You have to picture the action and believe it, otherwise it won't work out. So he pictured Fuller leaping up in his saddle and falling right over his horse's rear end.

Then, just as he was about to lower his Winchester and squeeze the trigger, something happened to ease the tension. Bunce made a slight fluttering motion with his hand which was intended as a signal. It could have gone either way.

You don't relax until you're sure. Watching for the signs Mav read the gunmen's body language and guessed the stand off was about to end.

Bunce nodded briefly and said, 'Remember I warned you, MacKinley. Next time things will be different. And I strongly advise you to get rid of that man Bolder before he drives you all to hell and back.'

'And I advise you to get your arse out of here,' Sam replied, tight-lipped.

Bunce gave a snort, turned his horse and rode away towards the hills. The two gunmen waited for a moment longer and then edged away from the creek and turned tail and followed.

'You see the way those venomous prairie rattlers were looking at you?' O'Leary said to Mav. 'Just like they were about to strike with their venom.'

Mav nodded slowly. 'I noticed quite a lot,' Mav admitted. 'I was looking right into the eyes of death himself.'

'Whose death?' O'Leary asked.

'That remains to be seen,' Mav replied.

At the table that night Sam MacKinley called a council of war. The two children complained that some of the kids had been nasty to them at school that day. Sam Junior was like his father: he didn't scare easily but he was worried because some of his friends said there was going to be war in the territory and everyone had to decide which side he was on. Sam Junior had gotten into a fight with the school bully and given him a black eye which didn't please Miss Angwin the teacher one little bit. Miss Angwin hated violence and her instinct was to spread the honeyed word of peace. Little Angelina, Sam Junior's sister, had also been threatened and sneered at but she just turned her nose up and ignored the bullies.

Riding home on their ponies the two children had encountered the Reverend Montague Means. He stroked his long white beard and looked up at them as solemnly as a judge about to deliver the death sentence. 'Well, now, children,' he said, 'have you had a good day at school?'

'Yes, sir,' said Little Angelina. She was in awe of the Reverend Montague Means and thought he must be at least a hundred years old. She had once asked her mother if Means was God himself!

'Can you spell out your letters, children?' the Reverend enquired in a syrupy tone.

'Yeah, we can both read,' Sam Junior replied less respectfully.

'Good, good. That's excellent,' the cleric said in the same syrupy tone. 'Please tell your father I'm coming round to see him soon. We must keep the peace in this town, you know, mustn't we, children?'

The children both agreed and rode on.

When they reported the conversation, Sam Senior laughed and muttered something inaudible, but Sarah hushed him up and commended the children on their good manners and their presence of mind.

Now at the Council of War, Sam tapped the table with his knife and everyone stopped talking. They knew that something serious was about to be said.

Sam gave an account of the incident up at Blue Gully and then addressed the future. 'Just wanted to keep you all informed,' he said. 'I see a heap of trouble ahead. That flannel mouth Bunce has hired two grudge men, and killers mean killing. When you let the cat out of the bag someone is bound to be scratched.'

From now on, he announced, there would need to be a watch kept on the horses and the ranch right through the night.

Later, Mav was sitting outside the bunkhouse with Daniel O'Leary. O'Leary was checking his Winchester and his Colt Peacemaker to make sure that everything was in good working order.

'Looks like the boss smells real trouble,' O'Leary said. 'This could be stick or bust for the ranch.'

'How long have you been here?' Mav asked him.

'Oh, I drift in from time to time,' O'Leary said. 'Like you I'm a tumbleweed. I generally go down south for the winter. Got a nice little woman south of the border. Real dark hair and eyes as bright as diamond stones.'

'So you aim to settle down then?' Mav said.

'Could be,' O'Leary speculated. 'I might even go back to the old country. Who knows?'

Mav was looking towards the barn and he saw a woman's form detach itself and come drifting towards them.

'You know what,' O'Leary said, 'I think I'll go inside and roll into my bunk. It's been a long day.' He gathered up his weapons and went into the bunkhouse.

Gladness hesitated and then made up her mind. She came forward and looked down at Mav in the faint light of the moon. 'Mr Mav,' she said.

'Miss Gladness,' he replied with a

smile. He half-rose from the bench. 'Why don't you sit down beside me here and we can talk.'

Gladness gathered up her skirts and sat on the bench beside him. For a time they sat peacefully together, staring up at the crescent moon. Mav felt a strange lump in his throat he couldn't account for and it stopped him from talking.

'I'm real worried,' Gladness said at last.

'I know,' Mav agreed. 'We're all worried, it's natural.'

Gladness gave a slight nod and Mav saw her clear, clean profile in the cloudy light of the moon.

'You remember back in Cimarron?' she said. 'You came and sat out there with me on the porch and I asked you why you always carried your gun with you and you said something like it was a habit and you didn't feel right without it.'

'I think I probably said I feel naked without it,' he said wryly.

He saw her smiling. 'But you're not

154

a gunman, Mr Mav. You'll never be a gunman.'

'You're right,' he said after a moment. 'I shall never be a hired gun. I shoot only when it's necessary.'

'I know that and I've seen it,' she said. 'But you could have got yourself killed up at Blue Gully today.'

'Sure,' he agreed. 'We could all have got ourselves killed.'

'Not only that,' she said. 'You agreed to fight bare fisted with that bully Bronco. What are you going to do about that?'

Mav considered for a moment. 'One step at a time,' he said. 'Bronco's big and he has a reputation as a prize-fighter.'

'Have you ever been in the ring before?'

Mav paused again. 'Well, once or twice I fought back east like when I threw my mother's lover out of the window. I guess you have to learn to duck and weave with a monster like Bronco.'

Mav chuckled to himself but Gladness didn't respond. 'He'll kill you if he can,' she said quietly.

'That's as maybe,' Mav said. 'But before that we have to think about your stage performance, don't we?'

'I don't want you to fight,' she said. 'I don't want you ever to fight.'

She got up from the bench and walked away into the darkness. Was she crying, he wondered. Was she crying on his account?

8

The day of the performance arrived. Mav didn't know what to expect. True, he had heard Gladness singing and it had sent a tingle down his spine. And way back east he had attended one or two performances by people like Lily Langtry and seen a few Grand Guignol type theatricals in which suggested rape, murder, and hauntings were popular. That was the extent of his theatrical experience.

Sarah MacKinley was very enthusiastic about the entertainment. Despite her tough life on the ranch she had a great love of the arts and wanted to expose her children to everything she considered good and wholesome. So she had booked the players and pressed Sam to let them use the barn. The question now was whether the people of Pure Water or 'Perdition' would attend in any numbers.

Sam MacKinley had pasted posters up in the town and most of them had been ripped down and trodden into the dust, which wasn't a good omen. Then a couple of days before the performance, two things occurred which shone a baleful light on the proceedings. The first materialised in the bulky form of Sheriff Bill Bronco who rode in one lazy afternoon and demanded to see Sam MacKinley.

Sam was down at the big corral, breaking in one of the horses. Mav was looking on somewhat critically. Sam and Mav had had a disagreement earlier about how you should make a horse more biddable. Mav said you should never go up and look a horse in the eye; you should approach it side on and talk to it quietly. Then, if you were patient, it would accept you and treat you as its master.

While they were sitting together on the corral fence, Bronco appeared and this time he was alone.

'Seen your posters up in town,' he said.

'Yeah?' Sam took off his hat and wiped the sweat from his brow.

'I don't remember granting a licence for you to give this performance,' Bronco said.

'That's because as I told you I didn't need you to,' Sam said again. 'Like I said the performance will be right here in my big barn. The people will sit there on bales. Why don't you come along with Mrs Bronco and enjoy the show?' Sam laughed. 'Could be you'll actually enjoy it.'

Bronco shrugged. 'That's beside the point, MacKinley, and you know it. I'm warning you. Some people in this town don't care for theatricals. Like it could lower the tone. Anyway, you have to pay big dollars to put on a show like that.'

'Tell you what, Sheriff,' Sam said. 'I don't need a licence but I might make a small contribution to one of the good causes in town.'

'Well, you should watch yourself,

MacKinley, in case something unfortunate occurs. You never know what might happen when folks get riled up in town.'

Sam put his hat on his head and peered down at the sheriff. 'You wouldn't be making some kind of threat would you, Sheriff?'

'I'm just stating the facts, that's all. Don't say I didn't warn you.' Bronco stared belligerently at Sam MacKinley and then even more aggressively at Mav. Then he swung his big black horse round and rode away.

★   ★   ★

The second thing that happened was that the Reverend Montague Means put in an appearance. He came like a messenger of doom, with his long black coat, his flat pork-pipe type black hat, and stroking his long white beard like an ancient sage.

'Good afternoon, gentlemen,' he called out genially.

'Good afternoon, Reverend,' Sam chimed out.

'Thought I'd come calling,' Means declared.

'You're always welcome, Reverend. Maybe you'd care to step into the house and take some refreshment. I'm sure my wife Sarah will be delighted to see you.'

'Well, that's very kind of you,' Means responded, 'but I think on this occasion I might just talk to you out here, if you don't mind.'

Sam climbed down from the fence where he had been perching. 'Had you something in particular you wanted to say, Reverend?'

'Well, yes there is, Mr MacKinley.' Means leaned on the fence and drew his long sensitive fingers over his beard. 'I heard what happened up at the gully yesterday and to tell you the truth it worries me a little. I know that no shots were fired which is admirable, of course. We don't want any more bloodshed now, do we?'

'Nobody enjoys killing,' Sam responded.

'Precisely, Mr MacKinley.' Means went on fondling his beard. 'But that's not the reason why I came. What I came about was the show you're proposing to put in your barn this Saturday.'

'Well, that's right,' Sam said. 'And I hope you'll come and enjoy it. We shall look forward to welcoming you.'

'We'll, I'm sure you will, Mr MacKinley, I'm sure you will. But I think you should know something. There's been a deal of talk in town lately and some people even claim that your show might go beyond the bounds of what is considered decent and proper, you know.'

Sam paused for a moment and then he threw back his head and guffawed. 'That's no problem to me, Reverend. I can assure you that everything in our show will be decent and clean. My wife Sarah wouldn't have it any other way.'

Reverend Means gave a brief nod. 'Of course, of course,' he said. 'I just thought I'd tell you what some people are saying, that's all.'

'And I thank you for that,' Sam said.

★ ★ ★

Something more sinister occurred on the Friday night before the show. Joe Basnett was a highly nervous man who got himself all wound up before a performance. Indeed, he had to in order to give it his best shot. So he practised on that old honky tonk piano well into the small hours of the morning and even then he wasn't quite ready for bed. He sat on a bale of straw and took a swig from the hip flask that gave him liquid comfort. Then he took another swig before stepping out into the night to cool off and reflect.

The sky was full of milky stars and everything seemed at peace up there at heaven's gate. Joe wasn't only to play the piano on the next evening, he was also doing a short piece from Shakespeare with Sadie Solomon, something from Romeo and Juliet. She was playing

Juliet and he was an unlikely Romeo. The scene had gone tolerably well in other locations but Joe was a perfectionist and he started pacing up and down, mumbling his lines over to himself. He knew he wasn't great shakes as a Romeo but he loved the words and, if you get Shakespeare wrong, he has a habit of coming to haunt you like the ghost of Hamlet's father himself.

As Joe paced stealthily back and forth, muttering his lines to himself he suddenly stopped dead. He had heard a movement close by. It was so quiet he thought his senses were playing tricks with him. So he stood with his back pressed against the barn, listening and waiting.

Then it came again, a faint rustling sound, and he saw two figures flitting like shadows across the yard towards the barn. They were whispering as they crept forward all hunched up and Joe Basnett figured they were up to no good. So he pressed himself closer to the wall of the barn and held his breath.

Now the two figures had paused and were holding a whispered conversation close to the door of the barn where in a few hours time the audience would be trooping in.

Joe Basnett wasn't the bravest of men, but he knew he had to do something immediately. It was too late to summon help: he was on his own. The two intruders were now inside the barn. When Joe crept closer to the door and peered into the darkness, he almost collided with one of the men, who had a gun drawn, while the other was bending close to a bale of straw.

The next second, two things happened almost instantaneously: a light flared up inside the barn and the man with the gun saw Joe and fired his gun point-blank. The shot came so close that it singed Joe's hair just above his ear. Joe sprang back and fell headlong with his face to the stars. The man with the gun rushed past him and turned to fire again. But it was a reckless shot and Joe was lucky. The other man darted out of the barn, trailing a fire brand, and the two made off down the trail, sprinting like a couple of March hares.

From inside the barn there was a small explosion and everything lit up in a ball of fire. Joe Basnett was no hero but his reflexes were well developed and he plunged forward and threw himself on to the flaming bale. Then he dragged it out and dumped it into the yard. Though he didn't know it, he was screaming and shouting as he fell.

The next instant someone else appeared. It was Daniel O'Leary. He had a bucket of water which he hurled on to the fire.

Someone else was shouting. People came running. Shots were fired from further down the trail. Someone hurled another bucket of water right in to Joe's face.

In less than five minutes the whole ranch was popping and moving. But the flames were quenched; that was the main thing.

Joe Basnett didn't remember anything

more because he tried to say something and passed out cold. Soon Sam MacKinley was on the scene in his night-shirt and he was carrying a shotgun.

Mav appeared almost immediately, fully clothed and riding on Huckleberry. He didn't wait to ask questions. He rode at a gallop down to the ranch entrance and on towards the town. The moon was bright. So he could see two riders ahead of him riding like the hounds of hell to get away. He drew his Winchester and steadied Huckleberry and fired two shots at the would-be fire raisers, but they were far ahead and he knew he hadn't much hope of bringing them down.

The next instant they had pulled off the main drag and disappeared between the numerous clapboard buildings along the way.

So he fired another warning shot and rode back towards the ranch.

★ ★ ★

Come sunrise, all seemed to be back to normal. Fortunately, Joe Basnett wasn't seriously injured though he thought he had been at death's door at the time. Now he couldn't stop shaking and talking about the close shave he had had with the grim reaper he had seen in a vision. Sadie Solomon and Queenie Caryl did their best to calm him down.

'You sure gave the frighteners on those two varmints,' Queenie flattered.

Sadie was studying his shaking hands. 'The point is,' she said. 'Can you still play piano?'

'I was practising just before those two fire raisers crept in,' he cried.

'Sure and you hefted up that bale and took it out into the yard,' Queenie said. 'That was a brave thing to do.'

Joe was flexing his fingers and blowing on them but a nervous man responds to a little flattery and he began to feel much better. 'I think I can play OK,' he said. 'Just as long as nobody takes a shot at me from the audience.'

* * *

The incident had actually been an excellent advertisement for the entertainment and long before the curtain went up the crowds were massing at the door — families, single men and women and whole bunches of children, all eager to part with their money. Sarah MacKinley and one or two of her close friends were sitting at the entrance raking in the coins and notes. Soon the barn was close to bursting and there were people standing at the back behind the bales where the privileged few were sitting.

Mav and Daniel O'Leary were on chairs behind the rigged-up stage where they could keep an eye on the audience in case of trouble.

'Don't think we have much to worry about,' O'Leary said. 'Not unless those gorillas want to fry the whole town.'

'I think you're right,' Mav said, peeking between a gap in the rather frayed curtains.

Then he became aware of Gladness standing close beside him, psyching herself up and ready to go on.

'Don't be nervous,' he said. 'You sing like a bird of paradise and nobody is going to stop you.'

'Thank you,' she said, giving him a curtsey and a smile.

'That woman sure has the hots for you,' O'Leary said after she had moved closer to the stage.

Mav heard but gave a dismissive shake of his head. He was looking out through a crack in the curtains again. The barn was full to bursting and the audience was getting a little restive already. People were shouting across to one another. Some were even exchanging jokes or insults but so far everyone was behaving reasonably well. There was no sign of Bronco or his wife or the Reverend Montague Means. But right in the middle he saw Obediah Bead and his wife perched on bales and, close by, Doc Blandish was sitting with a strange man-of-the-world smile on his face. The doc always had the air of a man who has seen everything and is surprised by nothing.

And now a ragged cheer went up as Joe Basnett stepped on to the stage and approached the honky-tonk piano. Strangely, Joe seemed to have lost his nervousness; he took a bow and seated himself at the piano. One or two cat calls went up and others said 'hush'. Joe raised his hands and brought them down on the keyboard and the concert had begun.

'It's gonna be good,' Daniel O'Leary whispered to Mav. 'Just like the old country, you know.' He winked at Mav in the gloom. 'I used to play the fiddle back there.'

It certainly wasn't a professional performance in any sense of the word but it was so rare in these parts that all the townsfolk were soon clapping and stamping their feet in time to the music. Joe played, if not like an angel, at least like a benign devil, and when Queenie Caryl came on everyone joined in with her and chanted along in the chorus.

'Just like Lilly Langtry,' Daniel O'Leary said to Mav in a loud stage whisper.

When Queenie Caryl announced the

next item which was to be a love scene from the famous play by William Shakespeare, *Romeo and Juliet,* the audience held its breath in anticipation until Sadie Solomon rose majestically from behind a bale of straw and then a few titters occurred. Someone whistled and another man shouted, 'Look, there's the Queen of Sheba'. Then, when Joe entered through the audience, there were howls of laughter and a whole chorus of 'hushes'. After all, Joe was several inches shorter than Sadie and when he climbed up on to the stage he looked like a shrimp about to confront a humpbacked whale that might swallow him in one gulp.

When he delivered the lines 'What light through yonder window breaks?' a gale of laughter arose and soon everyone was treating the scene as a comedy.

'I thought it was supposed to be serious,' Daniel O'Leary said to Mav.

Mav wasn't too familiar with Shakespeare, so he said nothing. He was looking out at the audience and he saw expressions of astonishment on a lot of the faces. Obediah Bead had an expression of anticipation and horror on his face but Doc Blandish was shaking with silent laughter.

The balcony scene might have been a disaster but Sadie Solomon and Joe Basnett had had a lot of experience and they started to play up to the audience and ham it up, especially when Joe forgot his lines and Queenie Caryl popped her head in from the side of the stage and gave him a loud prompt. Then, after Joe picked up on his line, Queenie turned to the audience and gave it a broad wink and that gave rise to a riot of laughter and prolonged thumping of feet.

Now it was time for Gladness to sing. Amidst all the laughter and confusion Joe entered again and took his place at the piano. When the laughter subsided he introduced Gladness as 'the Nightingale of the West' and she made her entrance with surprising grace. Soon the audience had quietened down and

173

Joe struck a few chords and Gladness began to sing.

'My, that woman has a real sweet voice,' Daniel O'Leary whispered.

Mav didn't need to be told. Gladness's voice held the whole audience as in a spell. It was so sad and poignant that it would have moved a heart made of stone.

'Where did she learn that?' Daniel O'Leary enquired in a whisper.

Mav was looking out at the audience again. Mrs Bead held a silk handkerchief to her eyes and Obediah Bead had his head down as though he couldn't bear the pain of it, and Doc Blandish was nodding with sympathy and approval.

When Gladness had finished, a huge roar of applause went up and it was obvious that the show had been an enormous success.

The love of entertainment is mightier than the six shooter, Mav thought ironically.

★　★　★

Everybody was congratulating everybody else on the performance. Sarah MacKinley was surrounded by well wishers, most of them women but there were a few men too.

'That was a great comedy,' someone said to Joe Basnett who replied, 'Thank you, thank you. I'm so glad you enjoyed it.'

Mav kept himself in the background. He thought there might be some kind of trouble. You never knew what to expect with a mean *hombre* like Bill Bronco. While he was standing close to the entrance someone spoke to him, and he turned and saw Doc Blandish.

'That was a remarkably good performance,' the doc said. 'Just the sort of thing this town needs. That Gladness woman has a real sweet voice. Could charm the birds off the trees.'

'Yes, she does,' Mav agreed.

The doctor came a step closer. 'You got time tomorrow, why don't you step up to my place. I have a few things I'd like to talk to you about.'

Mav nodded. 'I'll see if Sam can spare me with the horses,' he said.

* * *

After the performance nothing stirred in the barn and the whole place was becalmed. The actors had all gone to bed in their wagon and there were deep snores rising from the bunkhouse.

But Mav was far from asleep. He was thinking about two things in particular. First, there was the question of the would-be fire-raisers and the damage they might have caused. Then there was the question of Gladness and what that sweet voice was doing to his heart. As he stood at the entrance to the barn, looking towards the stage area, he could hear the echo of that beautiful voice which seemed to reach right down into his heart and pluck the strings there.

He even went to that honky-tonk piano and struck a few notes. I'm getting real soft and sentimental, he thought to himself. Then, as he turned, he saw the figure of Sam MacKinley framed in the doorway. Sam stood for a moment and then came towards him.

'Didn't know you play piano,' Sam said.

'I didn't know I did, either.' Mav struck another note and then closed the lid. 'My mother sent me for lessons when I was a kid but I didn't get anywhere. I was too busy shooting at other kids with pretend guns.'

'And now you're doing it for real,' Sam said.

'Only when I have to,' Mav said.

Sam nodded. 'There's going to be a showdown here. You know that, don't you?'

'That's what my jinx says,' Mav told him.

'That's a good jinx you got there,' Sam said. 'I've got myself a jinx too. And my jinx tells me you're gonna have a deal of trouble if you get into the ring with that prize fighter Bill Bronco.'

'That's my next big day,' Mav said.

'You aim to do a little training,

running and sparring, that sort of thing?'

'I don't think I have the time. I think I must work out my tactics as I go along. And by the way, Sam, I got myself an appointment with Doc Blandish. Is it OK with you if I go down to his place in the morning?'

'You got a tooth you want pulled?' Sam said. 'You know the doc was once a jaw cracker. I don't know if he ever qualified as a real doctor but he pulls teeth real good. He'll yank out a whole set in under one minute and even supply you with a new set of store teeth within the week, that's if Bronco doesn't do the job first in which case you probably won't need the store teeth anyway!' Sam gave a grim cackle of laughter. 'Doc Blandish is a real good doctor. But before he cracks open your jaw, make sure you got your shooter strapped on. You never know when you're gonna need it.'

'I'll make sure about that,' Mav assured him.

9

Doc Blandish was lounging on the back porch when Mav arrived. A tall grey haired woman of about fifty answered the door and looked Mav up and down like a solemn guardian of the temple treasures.

'You have an appointment?' she enquired in a down-the-nose tone.

'The doc said he wanted to see me after the performance last night,' Mav informed her.

'So it's not a medical matter?' she asked.

'I haven't decided yet,' Mav said. 'Could be ingrowing toe nails or a touch of the sun. You never know.'

The housekeeper lifted her nose and gave a snort. Mav guessed she couldn't be the doctor's wife. Housekeeper was probably a better word. The good woman conducted him through the old

179

style house where Doc Blandish was fanning himself with a large Japanese fan. Although it was still early in the morning, he was also smoking a rather fat cigar and taking an occasional sip of rye whiskey from a chipped mug.

'Ah, Mr Mav,' he said, creaking back and forth in his rocking-chair. 'Good to see you. Now, Molly, draw up a chair for Mr Mav, will you kindly?'

Molly, the housekeeper, pulled out a hard chair with a leather cushion tied on to it and Mav sat down.

'Now, sir,' Doc Blandish said. 'It's a little early in the morning. I usually take a bit of time to acclimatise myself. Maybe, you'd care to take a drink, a glass of rye, perhaps?'

'Thank you, Doctor. I think I'll just go for something a little softer if you have it.'

'Quite right,' the doc said approvingly. 'Molly, would you be kind enough to bring us a large pot of strong coffee?'

'Yes, Doctor.' Molly gave a slight bob and disappeared inside the house.

Doc Blandish chuckled, took a puff at his cigar and blew a cloud of bluish smoke into the air. 'Molly's a good woman. Takes care of me. Don't know what I'd do without her. Not much sense of humour but you can't have everything, can you?' He mused for a moment before shaking the ash from his cigar on to the floor of the porch. 'A man should look after himself, you know, especially if he's going into the ring with a bruiser like Bill Bronco. Would you care for a good Havana cigar. I have them shipped in especially.'

'Thank you,' Mav said. 'I don't smoke. Tried it once and it made me sick. I've never bothered since.'

'Quite right too.' Doc Blandish laid his cigar on an ashtray and took another sip of his whisky. 'Used to be a clean living man myself when I was young. Then I lost my wife.' He wrinkled his nose. 'When I say I lost her, I mean she died. After that I went to pieces somewhat. Somehow being clean living didn't mean much after that. And now it's too late to bother. I'll soon be joining her in the Happy Hunting Ground.'

He was still sipping his whiskey when Molly brought out a large pot of black coffee and poured Mav a generous mug full. When she'd vanished into the house again the doctor went on drinking and taking an occasional puff at his cigar for several minutes.

'You said you wanted to see me,' Mav reminded him.

'I did,' the doctor said. 'On two rather delicate matters, three in fact.' He leaned forward leisurely and tapped his cigar on the edge of the ashtray.

Mav nodded.

'By the way, I thought that show was quite commendable, last evening. Those players are a bit rough at the edges but it's what the people need and Sarah MacKinley knows that.' He held up his glass and said, 'There's no tonic better than laughter. You know that? A man should laugh at least twice a day. More if he can.'

Mav raised his coffee mug in reply.

'And that young lady, what's her name, Gladness. She has a voice like an angel. Reminds me of my late wife. She could sing like a bird. Could soothe the heart of an angry gorilla. Which brings me to my first point.'

Mav sat back in his chair and tried to be patient. In his professional capacity, Doc Blandish was brusque and sardonic. But this was a different man altogether, a man who liked to take things easy.

'I'm thinking about this bout of fisticuffs you're intent on. Of course the whole town knows about it and the whole town is looking forward to a second night of entertainment. Did you know what you were doing when you threw out that absurd challenge, especially after Bronco had knocked you out cold the first time.'

'You got a point there, Doc,' Mav said. 'But the way I figured it, I either had to face him in the ring or shoot him dead on the spot. And fighting him in the ring seemed to be the better option.'

'Hum,' the doctor growled. 'I'm not so sure about that.'

'I would ask a favour though,' Mav said. 'If you're gonna be there, perhaps you'd be good enough to stand by so you can patch me up when I fall.'

'Yes, sir,' the doctor nodded. 'I'll be right there in your corner, but I hope to do no patching up. I'll tell you, Mr Mav, I'm willing to place a bet that you will win this fight.'

Mav stopped drinking his coffee and gave the doctor a fixed stare.

'That may surprise you, I know, but I've been reading a few of the old papers from back East and I know something about Bill Bronco. He was a fighter, yes, but he was big and cumbersome and slow and he didn't last long. Now he's somewhat out of condition. He has a fist like a jack hammer and he can punch, but he's run to seed. Bronco's more than a bag of wind, but he's a bully and he doesn't fight fair. So you have to be fast and you have to weave and duck and wear him down. And don't let him get too close. Go for the solar plexus.' He paused. 'Have you ever been in the ring before?'

'When I was young I took a few lessons and I once threw my mother's lover out of an upstairs window but I don't claim to have more experience than that.'

'Well, we must hope that will be enough,' the doc said. 'You use your brain and watch out for tricks. Bronco's so full of tricks he could have been a conjurer.'

'I'll bear that in mind,' Mav said. 'But tell me, how come Bronco got to be sheriff?'

'That's a good question,' Doc Blandish said. 'They figured the town needed a strong hand and what they got was a bully. A lot of people want to get rid of him but they don't know how. Obediah Bead, for instance. Bead thinks that Bronco killed his brother but he doesn't have the grit to do anything about it. The Reverend Montague Means doesn't care for him either but nobody knows how to get rid of him. Which brings me to my second point . . . ' He paused to take another sip of his whiskey and another slow drag on is Havana.

Mav drank his coffee and waited. You don't hurry a man like Doc Blandish. The doc blew a cloud of bluish smoke into the air. 'When this fight is over, supposing you're going to win, some of the braver citizens might find the courage to elect a new sheriff. I wonder if you'd care to consider taking the job. I know you're inclined to be a tumble-weed. But maybe you should think about settling down.'

Mav sipped his coffee and considered matters. 'Now, Doc Blandish,' he said after a moment, 'I might have to take some time to work on that proposition. I just might not be ready yet.'

Doc Blandish was grinning behind his cigar. 'You take all the time in the world,' he said. 'A lot of folk in this town would welcome you.'

Mav drained his mug and poured himself another coffee. 'That's the second point,' he said. 'You said there were three.'

'Indeed.' Blandish flicked off his ash and rested his cigar on an ashtray again. 'The third thing I wanted to say is to do with the deceased Jed Arnold. You remember what he said just before he died.'

Mav nodded. He remembered the moment Jed had grasped his hand and spoken those fateful words, '*I want you to have it.*'

'That's right; he did want you to have it too. He told me so himself the first time I treated him after Bronco had knocked him out cold.' Doc Blandish peered into the bottom of his mug and saw with apparent surprise that it was empty. He took up his cigar and puffed at it again. 'I knew Jed Arnold as well as most people. He drifted in and out of town from time to time. But I knew he had a certain respect for you. Probably reckoned you as a fellow tumbleweed.' The doc gave a throaty chuckle. 'I know you went into Maisie's place and took a small bundle from his room because you thought that was what he wanted.'

Mav put his hand into the pocket of his vest and drew out the wallet he had found in the bundle. 'Is this what you mean?'

'That's probably it,' the doc affirmed.

Mav reached into the wallet and took out a piece of crumpled paper. Then he opened it out and emptied a small object on to the table.

'Well, my,' the doc said. 'What is this?' He produced a pocket magnifying glass and studied the object. 'Why this looks like silver, Mr Mav.'

'That's what I thought, Doc,' Mav said. 'In fact I'd place a bet on it.'

The two looked at one another in silent amazement.

'Now, Doc, I think you're a man I can trust,' Mav said. He straightened out the crumpled paper and put it on the table. Doc Blandish took the object between his fingers and studied it closely through his magnifying-glass. 'Yes, that's silver,' he affirmed. Then he looked at the paper Mav had spread on the table. 'Well, I'll be goldarned!' he said quietly to himself. 'You know what this is?'

'I figure it's a map,' Mav said.

'Yes, a map,' Doc Blandish agreed. 'Rather crude but quite distinct.'

'You know the place?' Mav asked him.

'I believe I do,' Doc Blandish murmured. 'I believe I do. Yes, there's some writing here. Did you read what it said?'

'Difficult to make out, but I think it says *Yarmindo*.'

'Yes, Yarmindo. That's what it says.' The doc looked at Mav intently. 'You know what Yarmindo means?'

'Can't say I do.'

Doc Blandish tapped the map with his finger. 'I believe this is a map of the old Yarmindo silver mine. Played out and closed down about twenty years back. But this chunk of silver tells me something, you know that?'

Mav held his breath for a moment. 'I believe I do. It tells us that Jed Arnold had a claim up there and he found another vein. That's what he's trying to tell us from beyond the grave.' Mav had astonished himself; he felt a kind of shiver all the way up his spine.

'That's what it tells us,' the doc agreed.

They sat staring at one another for a moment.

'You know where this silver mine is?' Mav said.

'It's up in the hills no more than five miles north of here. I went there once. A pretty desolate place, as I remember.'

'Well I think we should go up there soon and take a look-see,' Mav said.

★   ★   ★

When Mav got back to the MacKinley ranch he got another surprise. The

190

theatre company were loading up their two wagons ready to pull out. Sadie Solomon, as wagon boss and leader of the group, was supervising the loading and Queenie Caryl and Gladness were stacking things up in the load wagon. Joe Basnett was sitting on the bench outside the barn flexing his fingers.

When he saw Mav he made an effort to get on to his feet. 'Hi, Mr Mav,' he said. 'We're just about ready to pull out.'

'You got another engagement?' Mav asked him.

'Sure, we're due at Peace Ridge two or three days from now.' Joe was in high spirits because of the group's success the night before. 'We shall miss you, Mr Mav, unless you have a mind to come with us and learn to act.'

'I don't think that's quite my style,' Mav said, 'but thanks for the offer.'

As he turned he saw that Gladness was staggering under the weight of a bulky case, so he ran forward, steadied the weight and heaved the case into a good position on the wagon. For a moment they pushed and pulled, side by side, and again he had the strange feeling that he and Gladness had more than a little in common.

'So you're leaving,' he breathed.

She was half-laughing and half-crying. 'Have to,' she gasped. 'Sarah wanted us to stay but there are only so many people in a town like this, aren't there? So we have to move on.' Her eyes were wide and enquiring. 'Sarah and Sam want us to come back later, maybe in the fall. We might settle in for the winter.'

Mav wondered how they could possibly make a living on the road like that. It was like being some kind of Hungarian gypsy band.

Gladness was giving him a slightly mocking smile as though she had read his thoughts. 'What will you do?' she asked.

'I don't rightly know,' he said. 'Sam has offered me a job and somebody else offered me something too. I'm wondering whether I might stick around for a bit.'

Gladness's mocking smile turned to one of grim intensity. 'You know what's going to happen if you stay here, don't you?' she said anxiously. 'Sooner or later someone's going to kill you.'

Mav shrugged and pretended to be unmoved though he felt an unusual tightening in his stomach. 'We all have to die sometime,' he said fatalistically.

'Please don't talk that way,' she pleaded. He saw by the melting look in her eyes that she really cared.

'You won't be here for the big fight then, will you?' he said.

Gladness winced. 'I can't bear the thought of that huge man pummelling you with those big fists of his. I believe they don't wear gloves either.' She shuddered and turned her face away.

Mav sat looking at her in amazement for a moment. Then, without thinking, he stretched out his arm and touched her shoulder. It was like an electrical charge and they both felt it. She pulled herself away from him and hid her face. He took her gently by the shoulders and turned her towards him. She buried her face against his shoulder and cried.

'Don't put me through this!' she said.

Mav didn't know what to say. He just soothed her shoulder and kissed the nape of her neck. Then she suddenly sprang away and ran from him.

Mav was totally perplexed, He shook his head in dismay. When he looked again Queenie Caryl was standing over him with her hands on her hips. Queenie was a big strong woman and she looked like an Amazonian.

'Now what have you done, you big galoot?' she accused.

'I don't know,' Mav shook his head.

'You don't know,' she mocked. 'He doesn't know,' she shouted into the air. 'Why, you've done made that poor creature fall in love with you, that's what you've done.'

Mav stared at Queenie in amazement.

'Question is,' she said, 'what do you aim to do about it?'

★   ★   ★

Up in the big corral Sam MacKinley was working the horses with some of the hands. Another man was perched on the fence watching as the horses milled around. Every few minutes the other man pointed his finger at one of the horses and the hands cut out the horse selected and rode it away to another corral. Some of the horses were quiet and relatively docile while others were skittish and tended to buck to get the riders off their backs.

'What I need is a good cow horse, not too skittish but with savvy enough to be trained,' the rancher said. 'That one looks right.' He pointed to a skewbald on the edge of the bunch.

Now came the bargaining. Sam knew the value of every horse he reared and he was known as a hard bargainer but an honest man.

When the deal was settled they came down from the corral fence and Sam introduced Mav as his ramrod. Mav

195

shook hands with the rancher and they went into the ranch house to settle the deal with a glass of rye.

Daniel O'Leary was in the corral, leading the main bunch of horses into the pasture. Then he rode up to Mav and grinned down at him. 'You know what, Mr Mav, the boss man is treating you like a real gent, you know that.' Was there a tinge of envy, even mockery in his voice, Mav wondered.

'We've got a special assignment,' O'Leary told him.

'What's that then?'

'Just you and me,' O'Leary said. 'Sam wants us to escort the actors one day's ride just to make sure they're good and safe. Treat it like a day off and you haven't even started yet.' He laughed. Daniel O'Leary wasn't the most tactful of men but Mav liked blunt speech, so he wasn't troubled. The idea of escorting the actors for a day and then riding back the next day was quite appealing. Mav was still trying to recover from Queenie's revelation which had thrown him into a state of confusion. What am I going to do, he had asked himself a million times. What do I want to do? A more important question. Life was becoming very complicated!

★ ★ ★

When the actors were good and ready the horses were hitched to the two wagons and the goodbyes were said. Sarah MacKinley came right out to the buffalo horns to see them off and Mav and Daniel O'Leary received a few hoots and mocking cat calls from the hands. 'You boys taking a holiday?' one of them called out.

The route to Peace Ridge took them right through Pure Water and, as they started through the town they had a big surprise. A crowd of folks had gathered to wave them off, among them Obediah Bead and his wife and the Reverend Montague Means and the children from the school who were cheering and waving hats and white handkerchiefs.

Sadie Solomon sat up and waved back with a simple turn of the hand like the Queen of Sheba and Queenie Caryl called out boisterously to the kids. Joe Basnett gave a tepid wave. A great Shakespearean actor and piano player has to pretend to be modest even when he isn't.

'Look, here comes the big man,' Daniel O'Leary said to Mav as they drew close to the sheriff's office. Sure enough Bill Bronco was standing under the shadow of the ramada. He had a quirly in the corner of his mouth and he was wearing his big black hat, but they could see his eyes gleaming with hatred and resentment as he peered out at them like a predatory beast from its lair.

'You think you can take him,' O'Leary asked Mav.

Mav shrugged; he didn't want to think about it too much. 'That's in the lap of the gods,' he said as he tipped the brim of his Stetson in a mock tribute to the sheriff.

'I don't think he'll like that,' O'Leary said.

'There's a lot of things that *hombre* doesn't like,' Mav said. 'But a man has to take what he gets and riling him up might put him off a little. That's what they call tactics.'

★　★　★

They rode on quite leisurely throughout the day and reached a water hole O'Leary knew of towards sundown, where they pitched camp for the night. Joe Basnett was to sleep in the wagon with all the supplies and the three ladies would sleep in the other larger wagon. The horses were hobbled under a little stand of trees where they could be fed and watered.

Mav and O'Leary spread their bedrolls a little distance from the wagons where they would be close enough to keep a look out for both the horses and the wagons.

'You think those hired killers might care enough to gun down on us?' O'Leary asked Mav.

Mav sniffed the air. 'You can never tell with coyotes and wolves. They could sneak in and slice a man's throat before he has time to realize it.'

O'Leary chuckled and went off to take a discreet leak.

The three women had already kindled a fire and were cooking up something tasty. Sadie Solomon had a long experience of being on the trail and she knew exactly what to do. She soon had Joe Basnett hustling around doing everything at her command. They might just as well have been married!

When Sadie called out 'Come and get it!' they all assembled round the fire and tucked into her wholesome stew. Mav ate in silence, looking across at Gladness who was sitting on the opposite side of the fire. She looked sad and thoughtful and he knew why. Tomorrow, come sun-up the actors would drive on to Peace Ridge and he and O'Leary would turn and ride back to Pure Water. At least that was the plan.

* * *

Some time around 2 a.m. Mav turned in his bed-roll and felt the light of the moon shining on his face. But it wasn't the moon because the moon doesn't flicker like that. He and O'Leary had decided to take watch in case anything unforeseen occurred, and this was O'Leary's turn. Only O'Leary wasn't awake. He was sitting on the ground, nursing his Winchester and his head had drooped forward over his knees.

'Dear God!' Mav shouted as he disentangled himself and pulled on his boots. Then he heard the galloping of horses and knew they were under attack. And the supposed flickering moon were flames rising from one of the wagons, the one occupied by Joe Basnett.

At that moment Joe came screaming and beating against his clothes as he leaped down from the wagon.

'Quick, get the women!' Mav shouted as he ran towards the wagons. But the three women were already clear of their wagon. Queenie Caryl was grappling with Basnett in an attempt to subdue the flames and Sadie Solomon and Gladness were already hurling buckets of water on to the blazing wagon. But Mav saw already that they were too late. That wagon, full of supplies, was soon well ablaze.

O'Leary was dancing a kind of Irish jig and he grabbed his Winchester and ran out into the darkness to fire a few shots at the retreating figures. No chance. They had done their worst. There was nothing they could do except drag the unharmed wagon free and let the other burn itself out with all their supplies.

So they drew away and Mav made certain that the horses were OK. Joe Basnett said: 'My God, I might have been roasted in there.' In fact he had escaped relatively unharmed. Queenie had torn his clothes off and thrown her shawl over him to kill the flames. He was burned and groaning, but with the right treatment, he would probably be OK.

'What do we do now?' Queenie said.

'There's only one thing we can do,' Mav suggested. 'We have to go right back to Pure Water.'

'That's darned right,' O'Leary agreed. 'We've got to get to stamp on those wolves and coyotes before they stamp us out of existence. It's got to be the survival of the fittest.'

Mav said nothing. He was inclined to agree with O'Leary.

10

Was this the end of the road for the players, Mav wondered as they made their way back to Pure Water. But Sadie Solomon was a strong and determined woman.

'Hold your heads up high when you ride through town,' she said. 'Some folks might laugh, some folks might cry, but we've got to keep our dignity.'

Nobody laughed and nobody cried. When they rode into town on the next afternoon people came out to stare and one man shouted, 'Did you lose your wagon?' referring to the missing wagon.

Nobody replied.

Poor Joe Basnett was delirious with pain in the back of the wagon, so they drew up outside Doc Blandish's place and carried the stricken man inside. Doc Blandish was in his office carrying out some kind of scientific investigation when his housekeeper Molly showed them in.

'Lay the patient down right here,' he said with his magnifying glass still in his eye. He bent over and studied the suffering man. 'My, my,' he said. 'How did this happen?' Apparently Joe Basnetts' burns were more serious than they had suspected and being bumped about in the wagon for half a day hadn't helped either.

Mav told the doc what had happened and the doc gave a kind of snarl. 'Well, we'll see what we can do here, but you'll have to leave this man in my care.' And he got to work on Joe Basnett immediately.

'Is he going to be OK?' Sadie wanted to know.

'We can only do our best,' the doctor said. 'But one thing's for sure: he won't be playing Romeo and tinkling the ivories for some little time to come.'

★   ★   ★

When the dismal band got back to the MacKinley ranch everyone came out and stared at them in astonishment.

'Oh, you poor things!' Sarah declared after they had told her the story.

Sam MacKinley tightened his lips and squared his jaw. 'I could have foreseen this,' he said. 'And now we have no choice. We have to fight this through to the bitter end.'

Mav agreed. 'First thing I'll do is to go down to see that damned renegade sheriff before he does more harm. He and that Bunce are nothing but madmen.'

'I'd like to come with you,' Daniel O'Leary said. 'You have to face down a bully. It's the only way.'

'That's true Daniel, but this is one to one. So I must do this on my own.'

Gladness was looking on in dismay. 'Mav,' she pleaded. 'I want to come with you. I've faced bullies before and I know how to shame them.'

Mav put his hand on her shoulder and their eyes met briefly. 'I know you're brave,' he said quietly. 'I've seen it in Cimarron, remember.'

'I just don't want to see you hurt anymore,' she pleaded.

'We're going to win this one,' Mav assured her.

★　★　★

Mav mounted Huckleberry and rode down to the sheriff's office. 'Are we doing the right thing here?' he asked his old friend. As usual Huckleberry said nothing, but he twitched his ear and Mav took that as a hopeful sign.

Bronco wasn't in his office and Mav stood for a moment, looking into the cells. Nobody there at the moment, he thought. Then he heard a step and saw Bronco standing in the doorway that led through to an inner room. Bronco regarded him with a slow jeering stare. 'So you're back in town?' he growled.

Mav knew that Bronco must have seen the dismal but proud band riding through Pure Water. 'You don't get rid of a bad penny quite so easily,' he said.

'It's come back shining more brightly.'

He was looking straight into the sheriff's eyes and the sheriff was staring right back at him. They were like two fighters weighing in before a fight. Bronco had his barrel chest stuck out like that of a turkey cock and Mav was drawn up to his full height. The sheriff was a good four inches taller than Mav so anybody looking in through the door might have seen the picture as somewhat ridiculous but Mav didn't allow himself to feel at a disadvantage. He had learned from experience that when a man means you harm, you have to watch his eyes. Without meaning to, your opponent will give himself away and you'll know when he's about to strike. They say it's the same with snakes and wild cats!

And so it was at this moment, as Mav stared into Bronco's eyes, that he saw a kind of flicker. It was very faint but it was real and it said something to Mav. It said, 'This hombre is a bully and he's afraid'.

'I've come to tell you something,' Mav said.

'And I'm here to tell *you* something,' the sheriff replied.

'You know what,' Mav said. 'There's nothing a big bag of wind like you can tell me I don't already know.'

That struck home immediately. Bronco boiled up like an overfilled kettle. His clenched fists tightened and his eyes seemed to jump right out of his head. In another second he would strike out with his right fist and pound Mav into the wall. The wall would shake and collapse and the whole place would come tumbling down about their ears.

There was a moment of high tension but Mav would not back off. He kept staring right back into the bully's eyes. And little by little the tide began to recede. Bronco's heavy breathing started to quieten and he said, 'A man doesn't talk to me like that.'

'Well, this man has,' Mav said. 'And I'll tell you something else. This man will go on talking like that until things change around here.'

Bronco was still having difficulty with his breathing. 'That's when you get out of this town for good or when you drop down on the floor of that ring and don't get up again.'

'Well the bets are on for that,' Bronco said with a little more confidence, 'and I hope Doc Blandish is standing by ready when they shovel up what's left after I've pounded the hell out of you.'

'Listen, Bronco,' Mav said. 'I'm gonna meet you on that and I hope your buddies, particularly Bunce and his hired killers, are around. I hope they'll be ready to shovel up what's left of you, which might be quite a job.'

Bronco now stuck his thumbs through his belt. He had calmed down somewhat and Mav saw his belly shaking with laughter. 'Is that what you came to tell me?' Bronco said.

'No, there was just one other thing,' Mav said. 'If there's any more trickery and any more shooting around here a lot more of your buddies are going to end up stiff and dead. And that's not speculation, that's a promise.'

Mav went to the door of the sheriff's office and turned. 'I'll see you in the ring, Bronco,' he said.

★ ★ ★

They fixed up a boxing ring in what was normally the courtroom when the judge was in town. They roped off an area, attached the ropes to the wooden supporting-beams and arranged seats all round the outside for those who wanted to witness the event. Some of the businessmen in town sold tickets and, like the entertainment at the MacKinleys', everyone wanted to be there. There would, according to reports, be a large crowd — even greater than that at the MacKinleys' — since all the men wanted to witness the outcome of this great battle and see the blood oozing from the boxers' mouths and eyes. Enterprising towns-folk even placed bets on the outcome.

Though most people would have liked to see Bill Bronco hit the deck, the odds went strongly in favour of a win against the small man Mav. After all, who was this character with the woman-sounding name? How often had he been in the ring? Nobody knew the answer to that.

'You should bill yourself as Jesse Bolder,' Sam MacKinley advised. 'After all Jesse Bolder is your given name and it sounds a whole lot better for a boxer.'

'Well, since I'm no boxer, I think Mav will do. Everyone calls me Mav. So Mav I am.'

'That sounds like a name for a man who is already defeated,' Sam said. 'Now, listen, my friend, my advice is this: if Bronco knocks you down, you stay down to the count of ten. That way honour will be served and everyone will be happy. You might be bruised a bit but it's worth taking a few bruises as long as you stay alive.'

But Mav refused to make any promises. 'As long as I can stand on my feet, I'll stay standing,' he declared.

Daniel O'Leary agreed to be Mav's second. He would be ready with the towel and fan him at the end of each round and even throw a bucket of water over him if he passed out.

One thing Sam insisted on was that nobody should be admitted into the courthouse unless he agreed to check in his gunbelt at the door. The Reverend Montague Means volunteered to act as guarantor on the grounds that he didn't agree with violence of any kind and couldn't bear to see a man pounded to death in the ring!

Then there was the question of a referee. Though everyone was eager to see the fight nobody seemed willing to act as referee. When one man who had had some experience was invited, he said: 'No, thank you. I couldn't possibly stand between those two and, if I make the wrong decision, I'm likely to be shot for my trouble!'

In the end the old geek from the livery stable was enlisted. Though he was so ancient, most people said he wouldn't have much to do anyway, since it would all be over in less than two minutes.

* * *

On the night of the fight, Mav was sitting in the judge's room at the back of the courthouse. He could hear the crowds beginning to assemble. There was a good deal of hooting and shouting, rather like on the night of the show, but this was somewhat more boisterous and ribald. These people were baying for the sight of blood . . . his blood!

Mav wasn't particularly well dressed for the occasion. He was stripped to the waist and he wore jean pants with a belt and his feet were bare. As he sat flexing and clenching his fists, Daniel O'Leary slipped in through the door. 'Well now, how are you feeling?' he asked encouragingly.

'I'm feeling just great,' Mav said. 'Never been better.' They both laughed.

'What's it like out there?' Mav asked.

'Well,' O'Leary said, 'They're a pretty wild bunch out there like on Saint Patrick's day in the old country. They're all sitting there drinking and swearing at one another and placing last minute bets on the winner.'

Mav didn't bother to ask who the 'winner' might be!

'Most everybody's there,' O'Leary told him. 'Even the women. And Bunce too! He just came in with his two hired guns, except that they weren't wearing their guns. They must have figured they wouldn't need them.' O'Leary gave a nervous laugh. 'Sorry. That was a bad joke.'

So Bunce is there with his two hired guns, Jake Fuller and Smith Riley, Mav thought. He pictured them sitting out there beside the ring. They might not be wearing their guns but they were still just as menacing and tricky.

O'Leary went out to inspect the crowd again, some of whom were beginning to stamp their feet and chant with impatience. Then O'Leary opened the door again and said: 'Mav, there's someone special to see you.'

The next second Gladness was standing in the room. She wasn't crying and her eyes weren't red. She just looked happy and shocked at the same time. 'I've come to say I think you're very brave and I'm with you all the way,' she said in a bold but quiet tone.

'Sit down, Gladness,' he said, patting the chair beside him.

Gladness hesitated for just one moment. Then she sat down and turned towards him.

'Listen,' he said touching her hand. 'I know life has dealt you quite a bad hand and . . . I want to make things better for you.'

She was looking at him with her tender, kind eyes, and waiting. 'You do,' she said quietly. 'You always do.'

He grasped her hand. 'Before I go into that ring and whatever happens out there, I want you to know that . . . ' He faltered and couldn't go on. 'I want to ask you . . . ' Again he couldn't find the right words. Then it all came tumbling out in a rush. 'Gladness, I love you and I want you to marry me. That's if you care to.'

He looked at her in astonishment. Did I say that? he wondered.

She was looking at him with an expression of delight and astonishment. It was like the first ray of the sun coming over the mountain.

'Will you marry me, Gladness?' he asked.

'Yes,' she said. 'Yes, I will.'

And they kissed.

* * *

Gladness slipped out and it was time for the contest to begin. O'Leary appeared again. 'Are you good and ready, my man?' he asked.

'I'm more than ready,' Mav shouted. 'Lead the way to the Bengal tiger!'

As they entered the hall they were greeted by a great gust of noise: cheers, jeers, and laughter. Mav looked round in amazement. Though the faces in the crowd were etched with unusual clarity everything seemed strangely unreal.

O'Leary was close beside him. 'Get a grip on yourself,' he said. 'This is the big day.'

Mav knew O'Leary was right as he climbed into the ring and held up his arms like a champion. Did he feel like a champion? If he had paused at that moment to think of anything at all, he would have admitted that he felt like a damned fool and a scared fool at that. But there was no time for thinking. This was the time for action.

He went to his corner and sat on the stool provided. On the other side of the ring to the left of the stool where Bronco was to sit, squatted the overweight form of Bunce the rancher. To his left and right the two hired gunmen, Jake Fuller and Smith Riley, were sitting glaring across at Mav. They might not be wearing their shooters but they looked as though they had enough venom in their eyes to turn a man to stone, and no doubt that's what they wanted.

In the middle of the ring stood the old geek who was to referee the fight. He was dressed in his overalls and probably stank of horses, but he came over to Mav and chuckled down at him. 'You got any last wishes?' he asked in a high wheezy tone. 'Some sort of fancy coffin. They even got a line with gold handles. I figure you'd be worthy of that.'

Mav didn't deign to reply. 'Just as long as you know the rules,' he said.

The old man went away chuckling to himself.

Mav looked to his left and saw a band of his own supporters, Sam and Sarah MacKinley and all the acting bunch including Gladness herself. They were all doing their best to smile and wave with encouragement though none of them looked too happy. At that moment Mav could have wished that he was miles away riding on Huckleberry towards some other happier town, or, maybe, even to the sunny gold fields of California with Gladness. But he didn't have long to dream about that because a great cheer went up at the other end of the hall, a door was flung open, and the towering figure of Bill Bronco appeared. Bronco stood for a moment framed in the doorway with light streaming out all round him and Daniel O'Leary exclaimed: 'By Jehosephat, it's the Great Demon himself!'

Then someone sounded out a brazen note on a trumpet and all the Bronco supporters let out a great whoop of triumph. I thought they wanted to get rid of that bag of blubber, Mav thought.

When champions approach the ring they usually carry out an elaborate dance, weaving and jabbing and punching the air, but, though Bronco was reputed to have a good deal of experience in the ring, he just raised his arms and bowed left and right to acknowledge the cheers of his supporters.

'Don't let them put the frighteners on you,' O'Leary said in Mav's ear. 'It's just a few loud mouths sitting together. Just a bunch of hired shouters and rabble.'

Mav didn't have time to take that in. The next second, Bronco had hiked his leg over the rope and he was doing his best to perform some kind of jig in the ring. Mav breathed in as slowly as his rapidly beating heart would allow but he kept his senses together and he noticed one thing in particular: Bronco's legs were lardy and heavy and looked like grey crawling slugs. His helpers had had to hold the rope down so that he could cock his leg over it. Now he stood like a tower about to fall on a cockroach and crush it to death. It was a David and Goliath situation and Mav didn't have a sling or a pebble!

Nobody could say that Bronco was 'a fine figure of a man'. Sure, he was tall and broad, but Mav noticed that his belly wobbled as he raised his arms and shook his fists. That's the weak point, the Achilles' heel, Mav thought momentarily looking at that blubbery gut.

'Take care to avoid those mallet fists,' O'Leary shouted in Mav's ear.

Now the old geek was in the centre of the ring beckoning the two contestants over to him. He looked like a pygmy tracker beckoning to a huge tiger and a rather more modest sized panther.

Mav went forward and the midget held out his small but muscular arms to keep them apart.

'Now, you two men, I want this to be a fair contest. When I say break, you break. When I start counting the one standing backs off. You both understand?'

Bronco growled some kind of assent and Mav nodded.

The old geek brought down his hand and the bell rang, and the contest began.

Before a fight starts, you think about tactics and manoeuvres, but once the bell is sounded and you see your opponent rearing like a mountain before you, everything becomes blurred and your instincts take over.

Bronco lumbered straight towards Mav and threw an enormous bone-crunching punch which, if it had made contact, would have lifted Mav right out of the ring. Mav ducked instinctively and pulled to one side. You don't want one of those mallet punches to connect, his body told him as Bronco staggered forward and careered into the beam at the side of the ring. The house didn't come down but it certainly shook. The crowd shook too but with laughter. That was one to Mav. In a contest nobody wants to hear the sound of ribald laughter when he throws a punch that fails to connect!

Bronco turned and shook his head clear and came lumbering towards Mav again. His iron fists crashed out right and left but without making contact. Mav found himself doing a strangely unfamiliar dance to avoid those hammer-like blows. His body told him that he was a lot faster than his opponent and that was his only chance of staying on his feet. Wham! Wham! came those great fists, as Bronco wasted his precious energy and staggered to and fro to regain his balance.

Watch the eyes! a voice said in Mav's head. Watch the big belly, another voice murmured in contradiction.

Suddenly his body sprang to life as though unbidden. As Bronco's right fist hammered in, Mav's arm rose and brushed it to one aside. The next moment, Mav had delivered a lighting jab into the giant's belly and his fist seemed to burrow right in and spring out again. The giant gasped like a punctured balloon and rocked sideways.

A bell sounded somewhere in the background of Mav's mind. The old geek was urging them back on to their stools. But Bronco didn't seem to hear. He went on thrusting and plunging with those heavy fists of his.

The referee was doing his best to push the giant back but to no avail and several men had to jump into the ring, grab Bronco, and force him back into his seat — which was no easy task!

The mist was gradually clearing from Mav's eyes. Don't get too cocky! he thought to himself as Bronco glared at him from across the ring. Bronco was still puffing and growling from the effort he had put in trying to put his opponent on the floor and he must have been frustrated. Mav had survived the first round and there was a buzz of surprise and excitement among the spectators.

Watch his eyes, Mav thought as the bell rang for the second round. This time Bronco had sprung up with alarming speed and he came straight towards Mav like a steam roller out of control. Wham! Wham! Wham! went his fists, but now he wasn't swinging so wildly. Somehow or other, he had started to remember his old skills and his tactics had changed. Now, instead of looping in, his fists came out straight as ramrods and, though Mav kept ducking and weaving, one of them caught him straight on the head just above his right eye.

Mav's head snapped back as though a rocket had hit him and a shower of stars and meteorites exploded in his head as he staggered towards the ropes. He might have pitched right into the crowd if eager hands hadn't reached out to steady him. But now Bronco was breathing hot nauseous breath right into his face.

'Now I'm gonna kill you!' the brute snarled. 'Now I'm gonna put you out of your misery and kill you dead.' Bronco reached out with his left hand and steadied Mav's head for the knock out blow.

Mav's head was reeling as he staggered away from the hand and collided with a supporting post.

Bronco swung with his right fist as Mav started to fall. The giant's mighty fist struck the post like a bolt from the blue. The whole courthouse shuddered and the judge must have felt it from twenty miles away. The crowd gasped and reeled. And Bronco danced away with a howl of pain, shaking his fist and blowing on it. There was a roar of laughter from the audience.

Mav was on his feet again. He shook his head clear as Bronco lumbered in, howling with pain and fury. The big man was totally out of control. He floundered and bawled and floundered again.

Mav had that sudden drained feeling of a defeated man about to be flung into the depths of a dark well. This cannot happen, he protested with all his being as he struck out wildly at the giant's belly. One, two, three, and one again! Those fists were smaller and lighter than Bronco's but his knuckles were as sharp as desert rocks and Bronco gasped out a mixture of spit and fetid air and doubled up. A sudden light flashed in Mav's head. He can't win, he can't win, he thought. I still have a chance!

Now Bronco drew himself up against another supporting post and braced his body for what he thought must be the last killing punch. But instead of hammering in that punch, he suddenly changed tactics again. He unclenched his fists and started clawing the air. 'I'm going to rip your eyes right out of their sockets and leave them hanging down bloody on your face!' he bellowed as he reached out and plunged forward, Mav ducked right down as close to the floor as he could. The giant stumbled and came on staggering until he hung right over Mav for an instant. He was so determined to get his claws into Mav's eyes he couldn't stop. Mav braced himself and pushed up as Bronco fell across his back. Mav might have been crushed like a beetle if the man's weight hadn't propelled him forward. Bronco performed a kind of unintentional cartwheel and flipped right over on to his back into the front row of the audience. Though the spectators drew away in panic it was too late to get out of the giant's way and, as Bronco came rocketing down, several of them were trapped amidst a tangle of chairs. Bronco landed with a sickly crash on

228

his back facing the ceiling. He blinked and screamed with pain, made one feeble attempt to rise and extricate himself and screamed again. Then he lashed out involuntarily, made a last feeble attempt to rise, and fell back and lay still amidst crushed bodies and broken chairs.

There was a gasp of horror from the audience. Then a moment of stillness came with great shouts of mingled horror and screams from the trapped victims.

The old geek rushed forward to count the giant out but there was no need: Bronco lay completely unconscious and helpless amidst a tangle of chairs and struggling human bodies.

The old geek couldn't make up his mind what to do. He attempted to grasp Mav's arm and declare him the winner, but there was little doubt about the conclusion.

Mav stood gasping in amazement. The next instant his knees started buckling and he sank down on to the floor of the courthouse.

Then all hell broke loose. Men and woman rushed into the ring. Some tried to throw their arms round Mav. Some tried to kiss him. Some started to thump him on the back. Then someone else hurled a chair into the ring. That was followed by a bottle. After that came a stream of abuse, a mingling of cheers and shrieks and curses. Fists went flying. People hurled abuse and struck out at one another. A chaotic fist fight broke out in the courthouse. Someone was tolling a bell.

And the walls seemed to come down like the walls of Jericho on all sides as Mav blacked out.

11

Mav became aware of a painful hammering like someone was demolishing a house somewhere close by. The next moment, he realized that the hammering was in his own head and he was the house. The groaning he heard was his own voice but he could do nothing to stop it. My God, where am I? Who killed me? he thought in panic.

Then someone was squeezing cold water on to his brow and he came to and opened his eyes and saw the beloved face of an angel and the angel's name was Gladness.

'You're going to be OK,' she assured him quietly.

'What happened?' he managed to say.

'It's all over now,' she said. 'They're clearing the hall.'

The next moment the angel turned into a hoary old man with whiskey breath and it was Doc Blandish. 'How many fingers am I holding up?' the doc asked him.

'Three,' Mav managed to murmur.

'No permanent damage,' Doc Blandish assured him.

Mav struggled to sit up and a part of the roof seemed to descend on his head and he almost passed out again. 'Take it easy,' the doc said. 'Have a swig of this.'

The whiskey cut through the mist and Mav's head began to clear. When he sat up again he felt a lot easier though the sledge hammer was still pounding, if a little more distantly, in his head. 'What happened?' he asked, trying to look round.

He saw people hobbling around in the great hall. Some were whining. Some were even crawling about among the debris. There was a general atmosphere of quietening confusion and return to normality as after a great battle. But there was a circle of people standing back from him.

'Give the man air,' Doc Blandish said

and Daniel O'Leary flapped away with a towel to cool Mav down.

Then the old geek came bobbing towards him. 'You won the fight,' he shouted. 'Congratulations, young man! Now I can get back to my horses.'

'What happened to Bronco?' Mav asked.

'Well, he ain't exactly dead,' Daniel told him. 'Though he ain't too healthy either. I think the Reverend Means is giving him the last rites somewhere out there.'

That caused a ripple of grim laughter.

'Get me on to my feet,' Mav said. Several of the MacKinley hands came to hike him up. When he was standing square and reasonably steady, they supported him and got ready to take him back to the ranch.

'Why don't we give him a triumphal procession,' O'Leary suggested. 'We could perch him on our shoulders like Julius Caesar in the old times and carry him around the town!'

There was a hoot of approving laughter and someone said: 'Let's do that!' but Gladness suddenly intervened and put a stop to it. They brought Huckleberry up to the door and hoisted Mav into the saddle and took him back to the ranch where he could rest and recuperate.

Later Doc Blandish looked in to see how he was. The doc had been busier than he had ever been after the fight. Three people had been crushed under the giant's weight. One had a broken arm. Another had some sort of internal injuries caused by a dismembered chair. And one poor woman had flipped right over on to her back and had to be resuscitated by artificial respiration and carried away on a stretcher.

Doc Blandish's house had been converted into a virtual hospital, much to the dismay of Molly his housekeeper.

'I didn't have much chance to do anything for Bill Bronco,' the doc informed Mav. 'After I had given him the once over, Bunce and his boys cleared the way and carried him out. It took six men and they were huffing and puffing like Puffing Billies.'

'Where did they take him?' Mav asked.

'I'm not sure. They brought up a buckboard and loaded him on and carried him away like a dead man, only he was groaning and hollering with agony. The two gunmen fired shots in the air to keep people off. I've never seen Bunce look so blue and bloated. Thought he was about to have a heart attack. That was the last thing I wanted to deal with.'

* * *

After Doc Blandish left, Mav fell into the deepest sleep he had ever known and he slept right through the night and right through the next day. When they brought a warm drink to revive him, though he was still aching, he felt greatly restored. He was in the MacKinley ranch house and Sarah and

Gladness had cooked up a huge breakfast which he ate with relish despite his still aching jaw.

Then, to his surprise, Sam MacKinley came into the big kitchen and said: 'I hope you're good and ready, Mav. You got a delegation here to see you.'

Then from outside trooped a number of leading citizens, among them Obediah Bead and the Reverend Montague Means. They were dressed somewhat formally and carried their hats in their hands like small black pies.

'What's this?' Mav asked in alarm. 'Did someone die?'

'Nobody is dead,' Obediah Bead announced solemnly. 'Mrs Donovan is recovering slowly after being crushed but everybody else seems to be doing well after that remarkable shindig.'

Montague Means nodded in agreement.

'How about the sheriff?' Mav asked. 'Is he still in the land of the living?'

'The sheriff is none too well,' the Reverend replied looking smug and concerned. 'That's what we've come about.'

'You mean like he's dying,' Mav said.

'Not dying exactly. Just humiliated.'

The members of the delegation exchanged uneasy glances.

Obediah Bead cleared his throat. 'Fact is, Mr Mav, it seems the sheriff has left town. When I say left, he was sort of carried away in a covered wagon. Nobody could see him but everyone knew he was there.'

The Reverend Montague nodded in agreement. 'I went down to the office this morning and found the door open. The sheriff's badge of office was lying on the desk with his keys and there was a notice pinned up on the wall. It said, 'The sheriff is out at the moment and he might not be back for sometime'. How do you read that, Mr Mav?'

Mav made no reply. He was already way ahead of them.

The Reverend Means spoke up again. 'The way I read it is that Bronco is resigning his office. After last night he can't face up to his disgrace. That's why he left his badge and his keys on the desk. And that's why we're here.'

'This is our elected mayor, Mr Oliver Manfred,' Obediah Bead said, waving his hand towards an important-looking gentleman with large mutton-chop whiskers. 'Mr Manfred has come to make you a formal offer. We want you to take on the office of sheriff of this town. Isn't that right, gentlemen?'

There was a murmur of approval from all those present.

Mav stood up slowly and surveyed the faces before him. They all looked eager as beavers but solemn. Obediah Bead was nodding in anticipation.

Mav was astonished but he couldn't laugh because his body ached so much. 'I guess I'll have to think about that, gentlemen,' he said.

★　★　★

Sam MacKinley had been standing to one side and, when the delegation had left, he shook his head with a kind of world-weary expression. 'You know what this means. don't you?' he said.

'I'll tell you one thing,' Mav said. 'This is no fairy-tale ending. Bronco has resigned because he can't take the humiliation. When he starts healing, his biggest hurt will be that the whole town saw him lying unconscious and groaning in the courthouse and he'll want to take his revenge. Which means that he'll want me dead.'

'That is a very genuine point you made there.' Sam ran his fingers through the stubble on his jaw. 'So it seems you have some big decisions to make, my friend.'

Sam didn't spell them out and he didn't need to. Mav knew he couldn't stay on as Sam's top hand if he took the sheriff's badge and he knew he was by no means through with Bunce's hired gunslingers Jake Fuller and Sam Riley. Those two killers must earn their keep and that meant gunplay and probable death for somebody.

On top of that there was the future of the theatre company and more particularly that of Gladness herself.

The next evening, they all sat round the big pine table in the MacKinleys' living-room and talked about the prospects. Sarah Mackinley wanted the theatre company to put down their roots in Pure Water and set up a permanent theatre. There was an old barn they could use immediately opposite the courthouse. It might seat up to a hundred people and they could put on entertainments right through the year. Sadie Solomon liked the idea but she was hard-headed enough to see that it wouldn't make enough money to see them through. That was OK, Queenie objected, because they could set up some kind of business in town to compensate. But no immediate decision could be made since poor Joe Basnett was still recovering from his burns and he was entitled to have his say.

Gladness was very much on edge and Mav was still uncertain about their future together. 'Why don't we ride up to the ridge?' he suggested. 'There's going to be a big moon and we can go mad together.'

So they rode up to the ridge to spend a little time alone and the moon came up big and red as if to peer down at them. From up on the ridge, they could see the full length of the town as far as the MacKinley spread on their left.

Mav spoke quietly to Huckleberry. 'Now, Huck, we need a little help and advice here.'

Gladness gave a high laugh that reminded Mav of her beautiful singing voice. 'Why do you speak to the horse like that?' she asked.

'He's not just a horse, he's a friend,' Mav said. 'When you're on the trail you need someone to talk to. Otherwise you're likely to go plumb loco.'

Gladness laughed quietly again and then became serious. 'What are we going to do?' she asked in a low uncertain tone.

Mav pointed into the sky. 'You see those stars. You ask them; they'll tell us what we must do.'

Gladness looked up where his finger was pointing and saw two stars quite close together. 'Those two stars are close together but they can never meet,' she said sadly.

Mav got down from his horse and helped Gladness to dismount. He was reminded again of Gladness's sad past, how her husband and two children had been slaughtered in an Apache raid some time back. He knew she had been very unhappy at that time.

'Those two stars can meet if we want them to,' he said. 'It's down to the stars to make their own decision about that.'

They sat down on a flat rock and continued to stare up into the sky.

'Just before you faced that monster in the ring,' she said, 'you said something to me.'

'I remember,' Mav said. 'I asked you to marry me.'

'People often say things they don't really mean at a time like that,' Gladness said.

'That may be,' Mav replied. 'But I always try to say what I actually mean . . . and I meant that.' He paused for a moment. 'I remember way back in Cimarron when you told me what happened to your man and those two little children of yours. I know I can't be the same to you and I've never been married. Didn't think I ever would be, but I know what I want, and what I want is you.'

He reached out for her hand and held it tight. Neither of them stirred for some time.

'That's why we have to make a decision,' she said.

'I know,' he agreed. 'And I haven't a single bean to offer you. I'm just a tumbleweed.'

'I'll take you as you are,' she laughed. 'Except that I don't want to lose another man like that.'

Mav nodded to himself and watched as a thin scarf of cloud passed over the face of the moon. 'I see what you're telling me. And I know where it's leading me and what I want. It's just a question of choosing the right path.' He paused again. 'And there's something else I have to say. I do in fact have a little more than a bean in my pocket That man I rode in to town with, Jed Arnold, he left me a silver mine.'

Gladness jerked her head up and laughed in that lovely tuneful voice. 'That sounds like the pot of gold at the end of the rainbow.'

'Except in this case it could be a pot of silver. Jed Arnold discovered a new seam and before Bill Bronco killed him, he left it to me.'

'Does that make a difference?' she asked.

'Not a bit,' he said. 'Come next Sunday, we should ride up there and take a look-see.'

'Just as long as you don't get yourself killed,' she said.

* * *

'Tomorrow come sun-up, I want you to ride up to the Blue Gully with a bunch

244

of horses to make sure we keep our ownership there,' Sam MacKinley said. 'Daniel O'Leary can come with you. He's crazy enough for anything and you're pretty wild yourself. How about that?'

'Sure,' Mav said. 'What do we do when we get there?'

'Well, you just water the horses and let them graze for a while and then bring them back before sunset. I'm thinking of building a small cabin up there to make sure that that Bunce character doesn't horn in on me again. You could look around for a good place to build. Would that be OK?'

'Whatever you say, boss man,' Mav replied.

'I would go there myself,' Sam said, 'but I have business to attend to down here.'

So quite early next morning Mav and O'Leary set out with a bunch of horses at an easy pace. While they were riding, O'Leary jogged along quite happily talking about the old times in Ireland.

'You know we Irish are just a little crazy,' he informed Mav. 'Some of us believe in leprechauns and fairies, that sort of thing. If you meet a leprechaun he might foretell your future. But you have to treat him properly. Otherwise he might put a curse on you,'

'That doesn't sound too good,' Mav said. 'I'm glad I'm not Irish.'

'My imaginary leprechaun told me you were a lucky son-of-a-bitch to have met that Gladness lady,' O'Leary laughed. 'But he tells me you're gonna be all right. She's a mighty fine lady and he thinks you should settle down together and let the moss grow under your feet.'

'Is that so?' Mav said.

* * *

As they drew close to the creek, they noticed that someone had erected another barbed wire fence to keep out the horses. And another board had been put up which said: 'Strangers, keep out! Anyone passing this line might get himself shot at.'

A message is one thing, but close to the fence was an Indian style tipi in front of which was a fire with smoke curling up from it. Beside the fire two *hombres* were toasting something on a stick.

When they saw Mav and O'Leary and the horses coming, they rose from the fire Mav saw that they were well tooled up and one of them was wearing two pistols, cross draw.

'Those two mean business,' Mav said to O'Leary. 'Pity your leprechaun didn't warn you about that.'

'They don't tell me about every-thing,' O'Leary breathed.

'Just the good things,' Mav laughed. 'You boys been here long?' he asked the two cowboys.

'Long enough,' one of them replied with his hand on his gun-belt, not far from his gun.

'What's that to you?' the other *hombre* sneered.

'What that is to me is I think you're trespassing,' Mav replied.

'That's a big word — *trespassing*,' the first man said. 'This land belongs to Mr Bunce.'

'I think you got that wrong.' Mav looped out his lariat and threw it neatly over the board. Then he urged Huckleberry back so that the pole and the board were pulled clean out of the ground.

The two cowpunchers stared at Mav in surprise.

'Now, if you'll just be kind enough to rip up these posts and the barbed wire attached, my partner and me would be greatly obliged,' Mav said. 'Then you can throw water on your fire, take your tent down, and hightail it out of here.'

The two cowboys stared at Mav in disbelief. The one who had spoken first, the taller one with the cross draw, spoke: 'You can't rightfully do this.'

'I believe you're going to do just like I say,' Mav replied.

'And who's gonna make us?' the

other man asked.

'We're here to say you do,' O'Leary said.

The taller man made a move with his right hand but, before he could draw his gun, he looked up and saw that Mav had already drawn and his Colt was pointing right at his chest. Daniel O'Leary wasn't far behind and his gun was levelled at the other cowboy.

'Now, you wouldn't want to make a big deal of this, would you, boys?' Mav said.

The two cowboys looked perplexed.

'Are you the man they call Mav?' the shorter one asked.

'That's me,' Mav agreed modestly.

'We heard you put the sheriff on his back in the ring,' the man said.

'You heard right, except that Bill Bronco put himself on his back when he came at me like a wild beast.'

'That great bag of blubber has no style, no style at all,' laughed O'Leary. 'Now, I suggest you do just what we tell you, that is if you want to go back to

Mr Bunce in one piece.'

Mav was watching the taller cowboy and he noticed his fingers were twitching. 'Tell you what you do,' he said. 'You just unbuckle your gun-belt and let it drop. You hear me.'

The two cowboys exchanged glances but they weren't ready to die yet. So they unbuckled their gun-belts as Mav had suggested and let them drop.

'Now you kick them away from you, nice and easy,' Mav suggested and, after a pause, the two cowboys did as they were told.

'That's good,' Mav commended. 'Now you just heave up those posts, wind up the barbed wire, and load them on to the buckboard and take them back to Mr Bunce with my compliments. Tell him to keep away from the gully because it doesn't belong to him.'

'And, by the way, before you load everything on to your buckboard,' O'Leary said, 'you take down that handsome wigwam of yours and put it on the buckboard too. I'm sure you wouldn't want to lose that beautiful play tent.'

The taller cowboy looked riled but he just growled his annoyance.

When everything was done according to plan the two cowboys stood about looking naked.

'What about our guns?' the shorter one asked.

Mav was inclined to be generous. After all these men were only Bunce's catspaws. So he unloaded the handguns. The cross draw man had a couple of handsome Remingtons and the other a short-barrelled frontier Colt.

'What about the belts?' the tall one asked.

The gun-belts were loaded with slugs. Mav heaved them up on to his shoulder and said. 'Tell you what, you can collect these from the sheriff's office next time you're in town.'

The two cowboys growled again.

'Now you get on that buckboard of yours and ride right out without looking round.'

'Don't look round,' O'Leary said.

'Remember what it says in the good book. When Lot's wife turned round she was turned into a pillar of salt. We don't want that to happen, do we?'

Neither of the two cowboys did much Bible reading; so they were baffled. But they got the message.

12

Sam MacKinley was worried. 'That land belongs to me,' he insisted, 'and I've got the papers to prove it. My horses were up there years before Bunce moved into the territory. Bunce is nothing but an old time carpet-bagger. He thinks the whole range is open yet he wants the best chunk for himself.'

Mav had never seen Sam so fired up.

Sam remembered the summer when it was so hot that all the creeks dried up and Blue Gully was the only place where his horses could take their drink. Without Blue Gully all his horses and his whole business would have collapsed. 'Only one thing to do,' he said. 'We must build that cabin up there right away and keep Bunce out and go to law if necessary. He doesn't own that creek and he doesn't need it. He just wants to strangle us and run us right off the range.'

Mav was surprised to see his friend so wound up and angry.

★ ★ ★

'We should have done it long ago,' Sarah MacKinley said. Like most women she had a good practical head on her shoulders.

Mav was in the corral checking the horses when a man rode up to the ranch. Turning, he was surprised to see that it was the tall cowboy they had turned off Blue Gully the day before. Now he was wearing a single Remington shooter stuck though his ordinary jeans belt.

Mav was unarmed.

'Got a message for you,' the man said. 'It's from Mr Bunce.' He looked down from his horse and seemed to gloat. He could have pulled his gun and shot Mav right through the heart without getting down from his horse.

Sam MacKinley came out of the barn. 'Who are you?' he challenged the man.

'Nobody in particular,' the man replied. 'Just somebody who works for Mr Bunce and I'm just bringing this waddy a message and it's just for him.'

'What's the message?' Mav asked.

'Mr Bunce asked you to meet him just before sundown at the other end of town outside Maisie's place. He'll have two friends with him and he wants you to come alone.'

Mav grinned. 'Wants me to come alone? Does he think I have a post instead of a head or something?'

'Says he wants to make a deal with you,' the man said. 'Says he could make it worth your while. Says for me to tell you this is a genuine offer. Mr Bunce wants to smoke the pipe of peace.'

'If Bunce wants to make a peace deal why doesn't he come right here and talk to Mr MacKinley?' Mav said. 'And another thing, why does he need to bring his two side-kicks? Hasn't Mr

Bunce got his own tongue to wag?'

'I can't answer that,' the man said. 'I'm just bringing the message as he gave it to me.'

'You can tell Bunce that I won't talk to him unless he pulls out of Blue Gully. Without that there's no deal with anyone,' Sam said.

The messenger made a wry face. 'That's a separate deal. Mr Bunce didn't say anything about that.' He turned to Mav again. 'Mr Bunce said unless you come alone, the deal is off. He won't show.'

Mav nodded. 'You can tell Mr Bunce that I'll be there but I don't want those two gung-ho buddies of his, Jake Fuller and Smith Riley, to show up.'

The cowboy gave a slight sneer that suggested he thought Mav might have chickens' feet. 'I don't think Mr Bunce is going to agree with that,' he said.

'Well, now, Mr Bunce can take it or leave it. That's the deal. It's just him and me. I don't want to have to kill those two gun-happy bodyguards of his.

It might give the town a bad name.'

The cowboy turned his horse. 'I'll tell Mr Bunce what you said. Just remember to come alone.' And he rode away.

*   *   *

'Are you plumb crazy?' Sam MacKinley said.

'Well, I might be a little loco,' Mav agreed. 'That's just the way it is.'

'You know what's going to happen, don't you?' Sam said.

Mav considered for a moment. 'I know what Bunce wants,' he said. 'Bunce wants me out of here. Thinks I'm rocking his wagon a bit too much.'

'If you go into this,' Sam said, 'you can't go alone and that's for sure. Me and some of the boys will come along with you. Daniel O'Leary in particular. He's a useful hand with a gun.'

'That's very thoughtful of you,' Mav said. 'But if you and the boys come along the deal's off. One way or the other, we have to settle this thing. You

257

know it and I know it.'

Sam shook his head. 'I don't like this. Bunce always has an ace up his sleeve. But you could switch the cards on him.'

'How would that be?'

'You could ride down and see the mayor and accept his offer. If you took the sheriff's badge you'd be legitimate. That might make Bunce draw back on this.'

Mav chewed the matter over. 'That's a good thought,' he said, 'but I think it's a little too late for that. Before the mayor could swear me in it would be too late and Bunce would figure I'd got cold feet and ride back the way he came.'

Sam could see the point of that. 'I don't like this,' he said. 'Whatever happens I'm gonna be there not far behind you so that I can make a play when Bunce cheats on the deal.'

Mav settled for that. 'There's one condition I want to make,' he said. 'I don't want Gladness to hear about this. You understand me?'

258

Sam raised his eyebrows. 'D'you aim to marry that girl?'

Mav looked thoughtful. 'Sure, I aim to marry the girl but I don't want her to be a widow before we start life together. She's had enough widowhood for one life.'

Mav shrugged and Sam chuckled.

*   *   *

Mav worked with the horses through the day and, just before the appointed time, he strapped on his gun-belt and borrowed another Colt from Sam, which he stuck through his belt under his vest close to his left hip. Then he took his horse Huckleberry and mounted up. He rode into town keeping a wary eye out left and right. Just because Bunce said they were to meet outside Maisie's place it didn't mean a thing. That bastard could pop up anywhere and throw a slug at him just the way Bill Bronco had killed Jed Arnold.

When he got to Doc Blandish's

place, he dismounted and pushed open the door which was already ajar. The housekeeper Molly was nowhere to be seen but Doc Blandish himself came to meet him.

'Ah,' the doc said, reaching out his hand. 'Glad to see you, my friend. Is there something I can do for you?'

'Do you do embalmments?' Mav asked him with a wry grin.

'Who did you have in mind?' the doc said.

'Could be me or Bunce,' Mav said. 'Or could be anybody who gets between us.'

Doc Blandish frowned. He had caught something on the wind. 'Well, I hope it's not going to be you. I aim to visit that silver mine with you before either of us goes up yonder. Now listen . . . ' He stepped back and beckoned to Mav. 'I hope you know what you're doing here. You'd better take this.' He handed Mav a small one shot derringer.

'What's this?' Mav took the derringer and examined it closely.

'What you do,' Doc Blandish said, 'is you put this in your right boot in case of need. That one shot might be just the shot to save you.'

Mav weighed the small gun in the palm of his hand and then tucked it into his boot under his jeans. 'Thank you, Doc. That's a real friendly gesture. I hope I don't need it.'

The doc shook his head. 'I know somebody's going to get killed before sunset and I'd prefer it not to be you. I'd come along with you if I knew how to shoot straight.'

'I'm glad you don't,' Mav said. 'Every man to his own trade and you're a healer.'

He stepped out on to Main Street and looked right along towards Maisie's place which was a good way off. He mounted Huckleberry and leaned forward to talk to the horse: 'It's been a long ride, old buddy, and we've got a little further to go. So keep your dander up.'

Hucklebury twitched his ears.

261

Though it was late in the day and the sun was low, the heat was rising from Main Street in pulsating waves and it felt like an oven or the road to Hell. There was scarcely a soul about and, as Mav looked warily left and right, faces appeared like the Devil's imps in windows and doorways and then disappeared abruptly.

These people know something, Mav thought. The word's got out. Everyone likes a good killing or a public execution.

As he drew close to Maisie's place, everything seemed eerily silent. There was no sound of roistering or piano playing, no shouting or screaming, just a weird and uneasy silence.

He stopped outside Maisie's place and drew into the shade of the ramada. For a moment he saw the faces of the girls peering at him through a window and then they drew back and disappeared. Someone slammed a door.

'I guess we'll wait here a piece and see what happens,' Mav said to Huckleberry.

Then he saw a faint cloud of dust rising as a figure came riding towards him from the west. He could tell even from so far off by the way the rider rode that it was Bunce himself. Bunce was heavy but he knew how to ride.

Pity this has to end badly, Mav thought, but a man lives until he dies and that's all I can say about it. Then another voice spoke somewhere in the back of his mind: 'Stop philosophising and keep your nerve and your concentration,' it said.

As he heard this, the bulky figure of Bunce drew closer in a swirl of dust. Mav knew by the way he rode that Bunce had seen him and, when he was close enough, Bunce reined in his horse. 'You come alone like I said?' he bawled out.

'That was the deal,' Mav shouted back. 'We both come one to one.'

Bunce nodded sombrely. 'Why don't

we get down from our horses and go into Charlie Water's saloon along here, discuss this whole thing over a drink?'

Mav remained seated on his horse. 'What whole thing would we need to discuss?' he asked.

Then he saw that under his big sombrero, Bunce was grinning, but it was impossible to see his eyes, so Mav couldn't read his lips. 'I have a proposition to make to you,' Bunce said. 'Could be in your interest to consider it.'

'In that case why don't we discuss it right here and now outside Maisie's place?' Mav said. He dismounted and dropped down beside Huckleberry.

Bunce considered the matter for a moment and then dismounted with surprising agility for a man so heavy. They both stood for a moment, watching one another like two wary cats. Mav noticed that Bunce was armed but with only one handgun and he drew his own conclusions about that: the two gunmen Jake Fuller and Smith Riles weren't too far off, he figured.

'I was at the ringside the other night,' Bunce said. 'I liked the way you cut down Bill Bronco. That had real style about it.'

Flattery, flattery, Mav thought. Anyone could see that that had been nothing but a bludgeoning contest with scarcely any style to it. And he thought he saw the way things were shaping. If you think I'm open to flattery, think again, you big ball of slime, he thought.

'Bronco had what was coming to him,' he said. Now Mav could see Bunce grinning under the big sombrero and it was like the grin on the face of a wax-work figure.

'Well, then,' Bunce said. 'Why don't we shake hands and agree on that? Then we can go and see Sam MacKinley together and get things worked out for the good of the town?' There was something in the man's voice that was meant to sound reasonable and beguiling but wasn't quite right, like a devil pretending to be a saint. Bunce reached out a large paw towards Mav.

He must think I'm a real sucker, Mav figured. Perhaps the actual thought distracted him for a fleeting second, but it was enough. The next moment Bunce had fallen like a log right in front of him. It was a surprisingly agile movement for such a big man. Was he about to pray to him like he was the Buddha himself?

Then, as Mav looked down at the bulky form, he heard a shot from an upstairs window right across the street. They say you don't hear the one that hits you but there are exceptions to that rule. Something struck Mav like a mighty hammer blow and threw him right back under the ramada in front of Maisie's place. He knew he had been hit but he was still conscious. Though blood spurted from his upper chest he could see the gunman in the opposite window drawing a bead for a second shot.

I've been winged! Mav thought in amazement, but I can still use my gun. It was as though someone had taken over his body and was acting for him as he drew his shooter and pumped off a couple of rounds. The man in the window leaped back and then doubled forward again, firing as he fell. Then he flopped out of the window like a discarded sack of potatoes and slid down the ramada and fell as dead as a stone on to the dust of Main Street.

Where's the other one? Mav's racing brain raved at him.

And now Bunce was on his knees again. He had his Colt in his hand and he was loosing off a shot. It whined so close that Mav felt the heat of the blast scorching his ear. He fired twice at the bulky figure rearing up in front of him. The rancher was roaring and blaspheming as he fired again but Mav's shot got him right between the eyes and carried him back as though he had been struck by a thunderbolt. Bunce sprawled twitching and kicking for a moment and then lay still with one arm pointing aimlessly at the sky.

Mav's brain was racing. No point in hanging around for the fatal shot, he thought. So he pushed himself up on to his knees and crawled out on to Main Street. His strength was draining away fast but it wasn't over. As he fell forward close to Bunce's body he saw the other angel of death Jake Fuller running towards him and firing as he came. Mav managed to get his Colt up level and he blasted off a couple of shots but his eyes were blurring and he missed with both. Fuller rushed on and gave Mav an enormous kick right in the middle of his head. Mav reared up and rolled away and got wedged against the sidewalk outside Maisie's place. He shook his head clear and snarled. If I'm going you're going with me, he thought as he tried to fire again. But just his luck, the hammer clicked on an empty chamber.

Fuller roared and laughed as he kicked at Mav's gun which flew right off and landed on the sidewalk. Fuller stood over Mav like a crowing turkey cock. 'Now my brother Ben gets his revenge!' he shouted as he brought his gun down on Mav's head for the *coup de grâce*. The world spun round and round for Mav and he felt himself sinking right into the ground. But then he reached down automatically into his right boot and pulled out the little derringer the doc had given him. One shot! He fired blindly at the jeering gunman.

Fuller jerked and rose and then fell right over him. For a moment Mav was face to face with the dying man. Fuller looked amazed. Where did that one come from? he seemed to say. Then he rolled over and fell on his back with an expiring sigh.

At that point Mav must have passed out. When he opened his eyes again he was looking at Daniel O'Leary, who was holding a smoking gun.

Daniel bent down over him and said: 'Are you OK, buddy?'

Mav was thinking that was a damned stupid question, just right before he passed out again.

* * *

When Mav came to, Doc Blandish was probing around in his chest.

'Just you lie quiet and steady,' the doc told him.

'Am I dying?' Mav tried to ask but nothing came.

'You just lie still and I'm going to make sure you're OK,' the doc said. 'You do as you're told and we can save you.'

That was good news, anyway, Mav thought. It seemed that Smith Riley's bullet had smashed one of Mav's ribs and lodged itself within a whisker of his lung. Doc Blandish gave him a whiff of chloroform, took a stiff whiskey himself, and managed to gouge out the bullet. He held it up with his pincers and said: 'You'd better keep this on a chain close to your heart as a mark of remembrance.'

'Did I kill Fuller with that derringer?' Mav asked later.

'No,' Sam MacKinley told him. 'That was down to Daniel O'Leary. He shot Fuller just as he was about to shoot you.'

'Well, I don't believe in miracles but I guess one happened here,' Mav admitted.

In fact there had been a battle royal in the streets of Pure Water alias 'Perdition' at sundown that day. Bunce's men seemed to emerge from every doorway and every passage like lice shaken out of a moth-eaten blanket. But Sam MacKinley had expected this and he was on the scene pronto with his bunch. There was a good deal of shooting, most of it wild and inaccurate. Windows were smashed, water barrels were holed, men and women screamed and cursed, and a horse was caught in the crossfire. Luckily, it wasn't Huckleberry, though he did become rather wild and terrified.

The battle seemed to rage for an hour or more, though actually it lasted no longer than twenty minutes. That was until Bunce's men realized the boss man himself was dead. Then they pulled back and rode yelling and bawling right out of town.

Daniel O'Leary's blood was up and

271

he wanted to ride right after them in pursuit but Sam MacKinley said they'd done enough and that they must think about their buddy Mav, alias Jesse Bolder.

★ ★ ★

They say you reap what you sow and Bunce had surely sown the seeds of his own destruction. His wife, a quiet woman resigned to the vicissitudes of life, would not allow him to be buried on Boot Hill; she was far too proud and maybe too devoted to her bullying husband. So she had him laid to rest on a site with a good view over the ranch itself. Thus ended the days of Edmund Bunce, the rancher.

'He was a good man who let himself be led astray,' she had been heard to say.

The poor proud woman was soon to be disillusioned. Ranching was becoming less profitable and she had to sell the ranch and go and live with her sister somewhere back in Kansas.

The two gunmen, Jake Fuller and Smith Riley? Well, their remains ended up on Boot Hill and nobody cared about them enough to erect a cross or put up a headstone. As for Bill Bronco, he was never seen in Pure Water again. Some said he had opened a boxing arena somewhere far away. The truth is he went north to Colorado where he opened a gambling den and could be seen wearing a highly ornamented vest woven by a Navaho craftswoman. What they forget to mention was that he was always supported by two sticks and could scarcely move without them. Rumour had it that he wore a woman's corset and never talked about his boxing days anymore. He was, however, reputed to be quite rich!

Though Mav was a quick healer, it took him some time to recover completely from the wound in his chest, though Gladness cared for him day and night; she became like his 'Lady of the Lamp'.

Sadie Solomon and Queenie Caryl went into partnership and opened a coffee house and restaurant on Main Street. They called it 'The Sadie and Queen' and that went down quite well in the town. Everyone remembered the musical evening at the MacKinleys' place; so the two were treated as celebrities. However, they had not given up their dreams of success in the thespian world and Sadie scraped enough money together with a little help from Obediah Bead to purchase a small hall almost opposite The Three Brothers where they gave annual and sometimes biennial performances for the enrichment of the community. At the start Joe Basnett joined the enterprise. Sarah MacKinley let him have the old honky-tonk piano cheap. Under Doc Blandish's tender care he had recovered well from his burns. So he was, at least for a time, content. Later, he moved away to California where he was lost from view. No doubt he's still plonk plonking away on some broken down piano around Los Angeles way.

Gladness, of course, took her part in the annual performances since she commanded a large audience with her beautifully sad and sometimes joyful voice. In fact her tones became noticeably more joyful in the months ahead.

And Mav . . . In fact Mav never took up the offer of the sheriff's badge. He had other irons in the fire. Some of the citizens regarded Daniel O'Leary as the hero of the hour because he had killed Jake Fuller and saved Mav's life. So O'Leary was offered the badge and he accepted it. What happened to him later we may never be told. On the other hand, who knows . . . ? Daniel O'Leary wasn't an Irishman for nothing, and he had a lot ahead of him.

As soon as Mav was in the saddle again, Sam MacKinley offered him a partnership in the stud ranch.

'Time you stopped tumbling about in the wind like a dusty old tumbleweed,' he said to Mav. 'That's the way I see it. You like horses. I like horses. Everybody needs a horse. So why don't we form a partnership?'

Mav had his reasons for wanting to settle down. So he agreed. In fact, he had sold out his interest in the silver mine. After Doc Blandish and he had gone up to take a look at it, they both agreed that it might make them a fortune if they could work it. Though Mav had never cared too much for riches, he had never seen himself as a businessman. So he accepted a good offer which did, indeed, make the company that bought it rich. That was how Mav found enough money to buy his part of the MacKinley spread, which seemed to satisfy everyone.

Next spring Mav and Gladness got married. Unfortunately, things did not go entirely to plan. The Reverend Montague Means got himself more than a little boozed up. But Sam MacKinley took him to the trough and ducked his head right into the water. After that, the ceremony went more or less according to plan.

A bride likes her wedding day to go

well. So Gladness was slightly put out by the appearance of the dazed and half drowned pastor. However, she soon recovered and, no doubt, that was one reason why her voice became so much more joyful after she was married to Jesse Bolder.

THE END

We do hope that you have enjoyed reading this large print book.

Did you know that all of our titles are available for purchase?

We publish a wide range of high quality large print books including:
Romances, Mysteries, Classics
General Fiction
Non Fiction and Westerns

Special interest titles available in large print are:
The Little Oxford Dictionary
Music Book, Song Book
Hymn Book, Service Book

Also available from us courtesy of Oxford University Press:
Young Readers' Dictionary
(large print edition)
Young Readers' Thesaurus
(large print edition)

For further information or a free brochure, please contact us at:
Ulverscroft Large Print Books Ltd.,
The Green, Bradgate Road, Anstey,
Leicester, LE7 7FU, England.
Tel: (00 44) **0116 236 4325**
Fax: (00 44) **0116 234 0205**

THE VINEGAR PEAK WARS

Hugh Martin

Saddle tramps Cephas Dannehar and Slim Oskin, drifting through the Vinegar Peak country of Arizona Territory, help an old colleague out of trouble, and in doing so get themselves on the wrong side of scheming Nate Sturgis, the self-styled boss of Vinegar Peak. In a lead-peppered struggle between their horse-ranching friends and Sturgis's toughs, bullets are soon flying and fires of destruction lit — all part of the growing pains of a raw western territory shaping its post-Civil War destiny . . .

THE SEARCH FOR THE LONE STAR

I. J. Parnham

It has long been rumoured that the fabulous diamond known as the Lone Star is buried somewhere near the town of Diamond Springs. Many men have died trying to claim it, but when Diamond Springs becomes a ghost town, the men who go there have different aims. Tex Callahan has been paid to complete a mission; Rafferty Horn wants to right a past mistake; George Milligan thinks he knows what has happened to the diamond; and Elias Sutherland wants revenge . . .

LAST MAN IN LAZARUS

Bill Shields

When a town marshal is murdered by five escaping prisoners and his new bride is abducted, the killers think they have avoided the justice they deserve. But the dead man's older brother is Nathan Holly, a feared and relentless US marshal who is more than happy to take up the pursuit. Holly rides north with a Paiute tracker, Tukwa — a man conducting his own quest for vengeance. Both will end their search amidst the winter snows of a mining town called Lazarus . . .

DOLLAR A DAY

Chuck Tyrell

Real Lee is a scion of an old Virginia family, and fought as a cadet in the Civil War. Today, he's a gun for hire. Tom Easter enlists Real for gun work protecting some Green Valley settlers, at the cowboy wages of a dollar a day. Real is reticent, but accepts when he hears Wolf Wilder and Finn McBride are also involved. But trouble lies in wait — will a dollar a day do the job?